"It was a r...

Fay murmured.

"For me, too. But stay out of my part of town, debutante," Donavan said gently. "You don't belong here."

Her green eyes searched his gray ones. "I hate my life," she said.

"Change it," he replied. "You can if you want to."

"I'm not used to fighting."

"Get used to it. Life doesn't give, it takes. Anything worth having is worth fighting for."

"So they say." She bit down on her lip. "But in my world, the fighting gets dirty."

"It does in mine, too," he told her. "That never stopped me. Don't let it stop you."

She lowered her eyes to his hard chest. "I won't forget you."

"Don't get any ideas," he said dryly, flicking a long strand of hair away from her face. "I'm not looking for complications or ties. Not ever. Your world and mine wouldn't mix. Don't go looking for trouble."

Dear Reader,

At Silhouette Romance we're starting the New Year off right! This month we're proud to present *Donavan*, the ninth wonderful book in Diana Palmer's enormously popular LONG, TALL TEXANS series. *The Taming of the Teen* is a delightful sequel to Marie Ferrarella's *Man Trouble*—and Marie promises that Angelo's story is coming soon. Maggi Charles returns with the tantalizing *Keep It Private* and Jody McCrae makes her debut with the charming *Lake of Dreams*. Pepper Adams's *That Old Black Magic* casts a spell of love in the Louisiana bayou—but watch out for Crevi the crocodile!

Of course, no lineup in 1992 would be complete without our special WRITTEN IN THE STARS selection. This month we're featuring the courtly Capricorn man in Joan Smith's *For Richer, for Poorer*.

Throughout the year we'll be publishing stories of love by all of your favorite Silhouette Romance authors—Diana Palmer, Brittany Young, Annette Broadrick, Suzanne Carey and many, many more. The Silhouette Romance authors and editors love to hear from readers, and we'd love to hear from *you!*

Happy New Year... and happy reading!

Valerie Susan Hayward
Senior Editor

DIANA PALMER

Donavan

Silhouette **Romance**
Published by Silhouette Books New York
America's Publisher of Contemporary Romance

For a special reader—Peggy

SILHOUETTE BOOKS
300 E. 42nd St., New York, N.Y. 10017

DONAVAN

Copyright © 1992 by Diana Palmer

ISBN: 0-373-08843-4

First Silhouette Books printing January 1992

Printed in the U.S.A.

DIANA PALMER

is a prolific romance writer who got her start as a newspaper reporter. Accustomed to the daily deadlines of a journalist, she has no problem with writer's block. In fact, she averages a book every two months. Mother of a young son, Diana met and married her husband within one week. "It was just like something from one of my books."

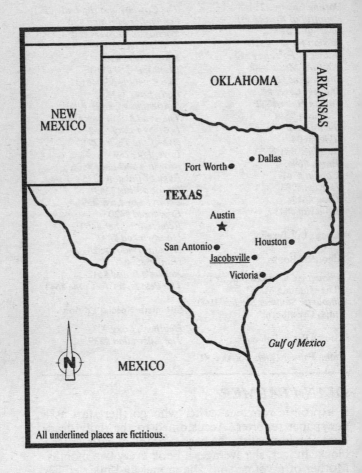

OKLAHOMA

ARKANSAS

NEW
MEXICO

TEXAS

Fort Worth ● ● Dallas

Austin
★

San Antonio ● ● Houston

Jacobsville ●

Victoria ●

Gulf of Mexico

N

MEXICO

All underlined places are fictitious.

Chapter One

Fay felt as if every eye in the bar was on her when she walked in. It had been purely an impulse, and she was already regretting it. A lone female walking into a bar on the wrong side of town in south Texas late at night was asking for trouble. Women's lib hadn't been heard of this far out, and several pairs of male eyes were telling her so.

She could only imagine how she looked in her tight designer jeans, her feet encased in silk hose and high heels, a soft yellow knit sweater showing the faint swell of her high breasts. Her long dark hair was around her shoulders in soft swirls, and her green eyes darted nervously from one side of the small, smoke-filled room to the other. There was a jukebox playing so

loud that she had to yell to tell the bartender she
wanted a beer. That was a joke, too, because in all her
twenty years, she'd never had a beer. White wine, yes.
Even a piña colada down in Jamaica. But never a beer.

Defiance was becoming expensive, she thought,
watching a burly man separate himself from his com-
panions with a mumbled remark that made them
laugh.

He perched himself beside her at the bar, his narrow eyes giving her an appraisal that made her want to
run. "Hello, pretty thing," he said, grinning through
his beard. "Wanta dance?"

She cupped her hands around the beer mug to stop
them from shaking. "No, thank you," she said in her
soft, cultured voice, keeping her eyes down.
"I'm . . . waiting for someone."

That was almost true. She'd been waiting for someone all her life, but he hadn't shown up yet. She
needed him now. She was living with a mercenary, so-
cial-climbing relative who was doing his best to sell her
to a rich friend with eyes that made her skin crawl. All
her money was tied up in trust, and she was stuck with
her mother's brother. Rescue was certainly upper-
most in her mind, but this rowdy cowboy wasn't her
idea of a white knight.

"You and me could have a good time, honey," her
admirer continued, unabashed. He smoothed her
sweater-clad arm and she withdrew as if his fingers

were snakes. "Now, don't start backing away, sweet thing! I know how to treat a lady."

No one noticed the dark face in the corner suddenly lift, or saw the dangerous glitter in silver eyes that dominated it. No one noticed the look he gave the girl, or the colder one that he gave her companion before he got gracefully to his feet and moved toward the bar.

He wore jeans, too. Not like Fay's, because his were working jeans. They were faded and stained from work, and his boots were a howling thumbed nose at city cowboys' elegant footwear. His hat was blacker than his thick, unruly hair, a little crumpled here and there. He was tall. Very tall. Lean and muscular and quite well-known locally. His temper, in fact, was as legendary as the big fists now curled with deceptive laxness at his sides as he walked.

"You'd like me if you just got to know me—" The pudgy cowboy broke off when the newcomer came into his line of vision. He became almost comically still, his head slightly cocked. "Why, hello, Donavan," he began uneasily. "I didn't know she was with *you.*"

"Now you do," he replied in a deep, gravelly voice that sent chills down Fay's spine.

She turned her head and looked into diamond-glinted eyes, and lost her heart forever. She couldn't seem to breathe.

"It's about time you showed up," he told Fay. He took her arm, eased her down from the bar stool with a grip that was firm and exciting. He handed her beer mug to her, and with a last cutting glare at the other man, he escorted her back to his table.

"Thank you," she stammered when she was sitting beside him. He'd left a cigarette smoking in the dented metal ashtray, and a half-touched glass of whiskey. He didn't take off his hat when he sat down. She'd noticed that Western men seemed to have little use for the courtesies she'd taken for granted back home.

He picked up his cigarette and took a long draw from it. His nails were flat and clean, despite traces of grease that clung to his long-fingered, dark hands. They were beautiful masculine hands, with no jewelry adorning them. Working hands, she thought idly.

"Who are you?" he asked suddenly.

"I'm Fay," she told him. She forced a smile. "And you...?"

"Most people just call me Donavan."

She took a sip of beer and grimaced. It tasted terrible. She stared at it with an expression that brought a faint smile to the man's hard, thin mouth.

"You don't drink beer, and you don't belong in a bar. What are you doing on this side of town, debutante?" he drawled.

"I'm running away from home," she said with a laugh. "Escaping my jailers. Having a night on the town. Rebelling. Take your pick."

"Are you old enough to do that?" he asked pointedly.

"If you mean, am I old enough to order a beer in a bar, yes. I'm two months shy of twenty-one."

"You don't look it."

She studied his hard, suntanned face and his unruly hair. With a little trimming up and proper dressing, he might be rather devastating. "Are you from around here?" she asked.

"All my life," he agreed.

"Do you . . . work?"

"Child, in this part of Texas, everybody works." He scowled. "Most everybody," he amended, letting his eyes linger pointedly on her diamond tennis bracelet. "Wearing that into a country bar is asking for trouble. Pull your sleeve down."

She did, obeying him instantly when she was known for ignoring anything that sounded like a command at home. She flushed at her instant deference. Maybe she was drunk already. Sure, she mused, on two sips of beer.

"What do you do when you aren't giving orders?" she taunted.

He searched her green eyes. "I'm a ranch foreman," he said. "I give orders for a living."

"Oh. You're a cowboy."

"That's one name for it."

She smiled again. "I've never met a real cowboy before."

"You aren't from here."

She shook her head. "Georgia. My parents were killed in a plane crash, so I was sent out here to live with my uncle." She whistled softly. "You can't imagine what it's like."

"Get out," he said simply. "People live in prisons out of choice. You can always walk away from a situation you don't care for."

"Want to bet? I'm rich," she said curtly. "Filthy rich. But it's all tied up in a trust that I can't touch until I'm twenty-one, and my uncle is hoping to marry me off to a business associate in time to get his hands on some of it."

"Are you for real?" he asked. He picked up the whiskey glass and took a sip, putting the glass down with a sharp movement of his hand. "Tell him to go to hell and do what you please. At your age I was working for myself, not for any relatives."

"You're a man," she pointed out.

"What difference does that make?" he asked. "Haven't you ever heard of women's lib?"

She smiled. At least one person in the bar had heard of women's lib. "I'm not that kind of woman. I'm wimpy."

"Listen, lady, no wimpy girl walks into a place like this in the middle of the night and orders a beer."

She laughed, her green eyes brilliant. "Yes, she does, when she's driven to it. Besides, it was safe, wasn't it? You were here."

He lifted his chin and a different light came into the pale, silvery eyes. "And you think I'm safe," he murmured. "Or, more precisely, that you're safe with me?"

Her heart began to thud against her ribs. That was a very adult look in his eyes, and she noticed the corresponding drop of his voice into a silky, soft purr. Her lips parted as she let out the breath she was holding.

"I hope I am," she said after a minute. "Because I've done a stupid thing and even though I might deserve a hard time, I'm hoping you won't give me one."

He smiled, and this time it was without mockery. "Good girl. You're learning."

"Is it a lesson?" she asked.

He drained the whiskey glass. "Life is all lessons. The ones you don't learn right off the bat, you have to repeat. Get up. I'll drive you home."

"Must you?" she asked, sighing. "It's the first adventure I've ever had, and it may be the last."

He cocked his hat over one eye and looked down at her. "In that case, I'll do my best to make it memorable," he murmured dryly. He held out a lean, strong hand and pulled her up when she took it. "Are you game?"

She was feeling her way with him, but oddly, she trusted him. She smiled. "I'm game."

He nodded. He took her arm and guided her out the door. She noticed a few looks that came their way, but no one tried to distract him.

"People seem to know you in there," she remarked when they were outside in the cool night air.

"They know me," he returned. "I've treed that bar a time or two."

"Treed it?"

He glanced down at her. "Broken it up in a brawl. Men get into trouble, young lady, and women aren't always handy to get them out of it."

"I'm not really handy," she said hesitantly.

He chuckled. "Honey, what you are is written all over you in green ink. I don't mind a little adventure, but that's all you'll get from me." His silvery eyes narrowed. "If you stay around here long enough, you'll learn that I don't like rich women, and you'll learn why. But for tonight, I'm in a generous mood."

"I don't understand," she said.

He laughed without humor. "I don't suppose you do." He eyed her intently. "You aren't safe to be let out."

"That's what everybody keeps saying." She smiled with what she hoped was sophistication. "But how will I learn anything about life if I'm kept in a glass bowl?"

His eyes narrowed. "Maybe you've got a head start already." He tugged her along to a raunchy gray pickup truck with dents all over it. "I hope you weren't expecting a Rolls-Royce, debutante. I could hardly haul cattle in one.''

She felt terrible. She actually winced as she looked up at him, and he felt a twinge of guilt at the dry remark that was meant to be funny.

"Oh, I don't care what you drive," she said honestly. "You could be riding a horse, and it wouldn't matter. I don't judge people by what they have."

His pale eyes slid over her face lightly. "I think I know that already," he said quietly. "I'm sorry. I meant it as a joke. Here. Don't cut yourself on that spring. It popped out and I haven't had time to fix it."

"Okay." She bounced into the cab and he closed the door. It smelled of the whole outdoors, and when he got in, it smelled of leather and smoke. He glanced at her and smiled.

He started the truck and glanced at her. "Did you drive here?" he asked.

"Yes."

He paused to look around the parking lot, pursing his lips with faint amusement when he saw the regal blue Mercedes-Benz sitting among the dented pickup trucks and dusty four-wheel-drive vehicles.

"That's right, you don't need to ask what I drove here in," she muttered self-consciously. "And yes, it's mine."

He chuckled. "Bristling already, and we've only just met," he murmured as he pulled out into the road.

"What do you do when you aren't trying to pick up strange men in bars?"

She glared at him. "I study piano, paint a little, and generally try to stay sane through endless dinner parties and morning coffees."

He whistled through his teeth. "Some life."

She turned in the seat, liking the strength of his profile. "What do you do?"

"Chase cattle, mostly. Figure percentages, decide which cattle to cull, hire and fire cowboys, go to conferences, make financial decisions." He glanced at her. "Occasionally I sit on the board of directors of two corporations."

She frowned slightly. "I thought you said you were a foreman."

"There's a little more to it than that," he said comfortably. "You don't need to know the rest. Where do you want to go?"

She had to readjust her thinking from the abrupt statement. She glanced out the dark window at the flat south Texas landscape. "Well . . . I don't know. I just don't want to go home."

"They're having a fiesta down in San Moreno," he said with an amused glance. "Ever been to one?"

"No!" Her eyes brightened. "Could we?"

"I don't see why not. There isn't much to do except dance, though, and drink beer. Do you dance?"

"Oh, yes. Do you?"

He chuckled. "I can when forced into it. But you may have trouble with the beer part."

"I learned to like caviar," she said. "Maybe I can learn to like beer."

He didn't comment. He turned on the radio and country-western music filled the cab. She leaned her head back on the seat and smiled as she closed her eyes. Incredible, she thought, how much she trusted this man when she'd only just met him. She felt as though she'd known him for years.

The feeling continued when they got to the small, dusty town of San Moreno. A band of mariachis was playing loud, lively Mexican music while people danced in the roped-off main square. Vendors sold everything from beer to tequila and chimichangas and tacos. The music was loud, the beer was hot, but nobody seemed to mind. Most of the people were Mexican-American, although Fay noticed a few cowboys among the celebrants.

"What are we celebrating?" Fay asked breathlessly as Donavan swung her around and around to the quick beat of the music.

"Who cares?" He chuckled.

She shook her head. In all her life, she couldn't remember being so happy or feeling so carefree. If she died tomorrow, it would be worth it, because she had tonight to remember. So she drank warm beer that tasted better with each sip, and she danced in Donavan's lean, strong arms, and rested against his mus-

cular chest, and breathed in the scent of him until she
was more drunk on the man than the liquor.

Finally the frantic pace died down and there was a
slow two-step. She melted into Donavan, sliding her
arms around him with the kind of familiarity that
usually came from weeks of togetherness. She seemed
to fit against him, like a soft glove. He smelled of to-
bacco and beer and the whole outdoors, and the feel
of his body so close to hers was delightfully exciting.
His arms enfolded her, both of them wrapped close
around her, and for a few minutes there was nobody
else in the world. She heard the music as if through a
fog of pure pleasure, her body reacting to the close-
ness of his in a way it had never reacted before. She felt
a tension that was disturbing, and a kind of throbbing ache in her lower body that she'd never experienced. Being close to him was becoming intolerable.
She caught her breath and pulled away a little, raising
eyes full of curious apprehension to his.

He searched her face quietly, aware of her fear and
equally aware of the cause of it. He smiled gently.
"It's all right," he said quietly.

She frowned. "I...I don't quite understand what's
wrong with me," she whispered. "Maybe the beer..."

"There's no need to pretend. Not with me." He
framed her face in his lean hands and bent, pressing a
tender kiss against her forehead. "We'd better go."

"Must we?" she sighed.

He nodded. "It's late." He caught her hand in his and tugged her along to the truck. He was feeling something of the same reckless excitement she was, except that he was older and more adept at controlling it. He knew that she'd wanted him while they were dancing, but things were getting ahead of him. He didn't need a rich society girl in his life. God knew, one had been the ruin of his family. People around Jacobsville, Texas, still remembered how his father had gone pell-mell after a local debutante without any scruples about how he forced her to marry him, right on the heels of his wife's funeral, too. Donavan had turned bitter trying to live down the family scandal. Miss High Society here would find it out eventually. Better not to start something he couldn't finish, even if she did cause an inconvenient ache in his body. No doubt she'd had half a dozen men, but she might be addictive—and he couldn't risk finding out she was.

She was pleasantly relaxed when they got back to the deserted bar where she'd left her Mercedes. The spell had worn off a little, and her head had cleared. But with that return to reality came the unpleasantness of having to go home and face the music. She hadn't told anyone where she was going, and they were going to be angry. Really angry.

"Thank you," she said simply, turning to Donavan after she unlocked her car. "It was a magical night."

"For me, too." He opened the door for her. "Stay out of my part of town, debutante," he said gently. "You don't belong here."

Her green eyes searched his gray ones. "I hate my life," she said.

"Change it," he replied. "You can if you want to."

"I'm not used to fighting."

"Get used to it. Life doesn't give, it takes. Anything worth having is worth fighting for."

"So they say." She toyed with her car keys. "But in my world, the fighting gets dirty."

"It does in mine, too. That never stopped me. Don't let it stop you."

She lowered her eyes to the hard chest that had pillowed her head while they danced. "I won't forget you."

"Don't get any ideas," he murmured dryly, flicking a long strand of hair away from her face. "I'm not looking for complications or ties. Not ever. Your world and mine wouldn't mix. Don't go looking for trouble."

"You just told me to," she pointed out, lifting her face to his.

"Not in my direction," he emphasized. He smiled at her. The action made him look younger, less formidable. "Go home."

She sighed. "I guess I should. You wouldn't like to kiss me good-night, I guess?" she added with lifted eyebrows.

"I would," he replied. "Which is why I'm not going to. Get in the car."

"Men," she muttered. She glared at him, but she got into the car and closed the door.

"Drive carefully," he said. "And wear your seat belt."

She fastened it, but not because of his order—she usually wore a seat belt. She spared him one long, last look before she started the car and pulled away. When she drove onto the main highway, he was already driving off in the other direction, and without looking back. She felt a sense of loss that shocked her, as if she'd given up part of herself. Maybe she had. She couldn't remember ever feeling so close to another human being.

Her father and mother had never been really close to her. They'd had their own independent lives, and they almost never included her in any of their activities. She'd grown up with housekeepers and governesses for companionship, and with no brothers or sisters for company. From lonely child to lonely woman, she'd gone through the motions of living. But she'd never felt that anyone would really mind if she died.

That hadn't changed when she'd come out to Jacobsville, Texas, to live with her mother's brother, Uncle Henry Rollins. He wasn't well-to-do, but he wanted to be. He wasn't above using his control over Fay's estate to provide the means to entertain. Fay hadn't protested, but she'd just realized tonight how lax she'd been in looking out for her own interests. Uncle Henry had invited his business partner to supper and hadn't told Fay until the last minute. She was tired of having Sean thrown at her, and she'd rebelled, running out the door to her car.

It had been almost comical, bowlegged Uncle Henry rushing after her, huffing and puffing as he tried to match his bulk to her slender swiftness and lost. She hadn't known where she was going, but she'd wound up at the bar. Fate had sent her there, perhaps, to a man who made her see what a docile child she'd become, when she was an independent woman. Well, things were going to change. Starting now.

Donavan had fascinated her. She tingled, just remembering how he hadn't even had to lift a hand in the bar to make the man who'd been worrying her back down. He was the stuff of which romantic fantasies were made. But he didn't like rich women.

It would be nice, she thought, if Donavan had fallen madly in love with her and started searching for her. That would be improbable, though, since he didn't have a clue as to her real identity. She didn't know his, either, come to think of it; all she knew was what he did for a living. But he could have been stretching the truth a little. He hadn't sounded quite forceful when he'd said he was a foreman.

Well, it didn't really matter, she thought sadly. She'd never see him again. But it had been a memorable meeting altogether, and she knew she'd never forget him. Not ever.

Chapter Two

The feedlot office was quiet, and Fay York was grateful for the respite. It had been a hectic two weeks since she started this, her first job. She was still faintly amazed at her own courage and grit, because she'd never thought she'd be able to actually do it. She'd surprised her Uncle Henry as much as herself when she'd announced her plans to get a job and become independent until her inheritance came through.

It had been because of Donavan that she'd done it. Her evening with him had changed her life. He'd made it possible for her to believe in herself. He'd given her a kind of self-confidence that she hadn't thought possible.

But it hadn't been easy, and she'd been scared to death the morning she'd walked into the office of the gigantic Ballenger feedlot to ask for a job.

Barry Holman, the local attorney who was to handle her inheritance, had suggested that she see Justin Ballenger about work, because his secretary was out having a baby and Calhoun Ballenger's wife, Abby, had been reluctantly filling in.

She could still remember her shock when she'd gone to Mr. Holman to ask for a living allowance until her inheritance came through, something that would give her a little independence from her overbearing uncle.

That was when the blow fell. "I'm sorry," Holman said. "But there's no provision for any living allowance. According to the terms of the will, you can't inherit until you're twenty-one. Until that time, the executor of your parents' estate has total control of your money."

She gasped. "You mean I don't have any money unless Uncle Henry gives it to me?"

"I'm afraid so," he said. "I realize it probably seems terribly unfair to you, Fay, but your parents must have thought they were doing the right thing."

"I can't believe it," she said, feeling sick. She wrapped her arms around her body. "What will I do?"

"What you originally planned. Go ahead and get a job. You'll only need it for a couple of weeks, until you get your inheritance."

The statement helped her fight out of her misery. Involuntarily, she smiled, liking the blond attorney. He was in his early thirties, very good-looking and successful. He was married, because on his desk was a photograph of a young woman with long, brown hair holding a baby.

"Thank you," she said.

"Oh, it's my pleasure. Don't worry, you won't even have to look far for a job. I just happen to know of an opening. Know anything about cattle?"

She hesitated. "Not really."

"Do you mind working around them?"

"Not if I don't have to brand them," she murmured dryly.

He laughed. "It won't come to that. The Ballenger brothers are looking for a temporary secretary. Their full-time one was pregnant and just had a complicated delivery. She'll be out about two months and they're looking for someone to fill in. Calhoun Ballenger's wife has been trying to handle it, but you'd be a godsend right now. Can you type?"

"Oh, yes," she said. "I can handle a computer, too. I took several college courses before my parents died and I had to come out here to comply with the terms of their will."

"Good!"

"But surely they've found someone . . ."

"There aren't that many people available for part-time work," he said. "Mostly high-school students, and they don't like the environment that goes with the job.''

She grinned. "I won't care, as long as I make enough to pay my rent.''

"You will. Here.'' He scribbled an address. "Go and see Justin or Calhoun. Tell them I sent you. Trust me,'' he added, rising to shake hands with her. "You'll like them.''

"I hope so. I sure don't like my uncle much at the moment.''

He nodded. "I can understand that. But Henry isn't a bad man, you know. And there could be more to this than meets the eye,'' he added reluctantly.

That statement gave her cold chills. The way Uncle Henry had been throwing her headlong at a rich bachelor friend of his made her uneasy. "I suppose so.'' She hesitated. "Do you know just how my uncle's been managing my affairs in the past two months?''

"Not yet,'' Barry Holman replied. "I've asked for an accounting, but he's refused to turn over any documents to me until the day you turn twenty-one.''

"That doesn't sound promising,'' she said nervously. "I understood my father to say he had at least two million dollars tied up in trust for me. Surely Uncle Henry couldn't have gone through that in a few weeks, could he?''

"I hardly think so," he assured her. "Don't worry. Everything will be all right. Go and see the Ballengers. Good luck."

"I think I'll need it, but thanks for your help," she said as she left the office.

The Ballenger feedlot was a mammoth operation. During the short time she'd been in Jacobsville, Fay had never gotten a good look at it. Now, up close, the sheer enormity of it was staggering. So was the relative cleanliness of the operation and the attention to sanitation.

It was Justin Ballenger who interviewed her. He was tall and rangy, not at all handsome, but kind and courteous.

"You understand that this would only be a temporary job?" he emphasized, leaning forward. "Our secretary, Nita, is only going to be out long enough to recuperate from her C-section and have a few weeks with their new baby."

"Yes, Mr. Holman told me about that," Fay said. "I don't mind. I only need something temporary until I get used to being on my own. I was living with my uncle but the situation was pretty uncomfortable." Without meaning to, she went on to explain what had happened, finding in Justin a sympathetic listener.

Justin's dark eyes narrowed. "Your uncle is a mercenary man. I think you did the right thing. Make sure Barry keeps a close watch on your holdings."

"He's doing that." She gnawed her lower lip worriedly. "You won't mention it to anyone...?"

"It's nobody's business but yours," he agreed. "As far as we know, you're strictly a working girl who had a minor disagreement with her kin. Fair enough?"

"Yes, sir," she said, smiling. "I'm not really much more than a working girl, since everything is tied up in trust. But only for a few more weeks." She smiled. "Money doesn't really mean that much to me. Honestly I'd rather marry someone who loved me than someone who just wanted an easy life."

"You're a wise girl," he replied quietly. "Shelby and I both felt like that. We're not poor, but it wouldn't matter if we were. We have each other, and our boys. We're very lucky."

She smiled, because she'd heard about Shelby Ballenger and the circumstances that had finally led to her marriage to Justin. It was a real love story. "Maybe I'll get lucky like that one day," she said, thinking about Donavan.

"Well, if you want the job under those conditions, it's yours," he said after a minute. "Welcome aboard. Come on and I'll introduce you to my brother."

He preceded her down the hall, where a tall blond man was poring over figures on sheets of paper scattered all over his desk.

"This is Fay York," he said, introducing her. "Fay, my brother, Calhoun."

"Nice to meet you," she said sincerely, and shook hands. "I hope I can help you keep things in order while Nita's away."

"Abby will get down and kiss your shoes," Calhoun assured her. "She's been trying to keep one of our boys in school and the other two in day care and take care of the house while she worked in Nita's place this week. She's already threatened to open all the gates if we didn't do something to help her."

"I'm glad I needed a job, then," she said.

"So are we."

Abby came barreling in with an armload of files, her black hair askew around her face, her blue-gray eyes wide and curious when they met Fay's green ones.

"Please be my replacement," she said with such fervor that Fay laughed helplessly. "Do you take bribes? I can get you real chocolate truffles and mocha ice cream . . ."

"No need. I've already accepted the job while Nita is out with her baby," Fay assured the other woman.

"Oh, thank *God!*" she sighed, dropping the files on her husband's desk. She grinned at Calhoun. "Thank you, too, darling. I'll make you a big beef stew for dinner, with homemade rolls."

"Don't just stand there, go home!" he burst out. He grinned sheepishly at Fay. "She makes the best rolls in town. I've been eating hot dogs for so many days that I bark, because it's all I can cook! This has been hard on my stomach."

"And on my stamina." Abby laughed. "The boys have missed me. Well, I'll show you what to do, Fay, then I'll rush right home and start dough rising."

Fay followed her back to the desk out front and listened carefully and made notes while Abby briefed her on the routine and showed her how to fill in the forms. She went over the basics of feedlot operation as well, so that Fay would understand what she was doing.

"You make it sound very easy, but it isn't, is it?"

"No," Abby agreed. "Especially when you deal with some of our clients. J. D. Langley alone is enough to make a saint throw in the towel."

"Is he a rancher?"

"He's a..." Abby cleared her throat. "Yes, he's a rancher. But most of the cattle he deals in are other people's. He's general manager of the Mesa Blanco ranch combine."

"I don't know much about ranching, but I've heard of them."

"Most everybody has. J.D.'s good at his job, don't get me wrong, but he's a perfectionist when it comes to diet and handling of cattle. He saw one of the men use a cattle prod on some of his stock once and he jumped the man, right over a rail. We can't afford to turn down his business, but he makes things difficult. You'll find that out for yourself. Nobody crosses J.D. around Jacobsville."

"Is he rich?"

"No. He has plenty of power because of the job he does for Mesa Blanco, but it's his temperament that makes people jump when he speaks. J.D. would be arrogant in rags. He's just that kind of man."

Abby's description brought to mind another man, a rangy cowboy who'd given her the most magical evening of her life. She smiled sadly, thinking that she'd probably never see him again. Walking into that bar had been an act of desperation and bravado. She'd never have the nerve to do it twice. It would look as if she were chasing him, and he'd said at the time that there was no future in it. She'd driven by the bar two or three times, but she couldn't manage enough courage to go in again.

"Is Mr. Langley married?" Fay asked.

"There's no woman brave enough, anywhere," Abby said shortly. "His father's marriage soured him on women. He's been something of a playboy in past years, but he's settled somewhat since he's been managing the Mesa Blanco companies. There's a new president of the company who's a hard-line conservative, so J.D.'s toned down his playboy image. There's talk of the president giving that job to a man who's married and settled and has kids. The only child in J.D.'s life, ever, is a nephew in Houston, his sister's child. His sister died." She shook her head. "I can't really imagine J.D. with a child. He isn't the fatherly type."

"Is he really that bad?"

Abby nodded. "He was always difficult. But his father's remarriage, and then his death, left scars. These days, he's a dangerous man to be around, even for other men. Calhoun leaves the office when he's due to check on his stock. Justin seems to like him, but Calhoun almost came to blows with him once."

"Is he here very often?" Fay asked with obvious reluctance.

"Every other week, like clockwork."

"Then I'm very glad I won't be around long," she said with feeling.

Abby laughed. "Not to worry. He'll barely notice you. It's Calhoun and Justin who get the range language."

"I feel better already," she said.

Her first day was tiring, but by the end of it she knew how many records had to be compiled each day on the individual lots of cattle. She learned volumes about weight gain ratios, feed supplements, veterinary services, daily chores and form filing. If it sounded simple just to feed cattle, it wasn't. There were hundreds of details to be attended to, and printouts of daily averages to be compiled for clients.

As the days went by and she fell into the routine of the job, Fay couldn't help but wonder if Donavan ever came here. He was foreman for a ranch, he'd told her. If that ranch had feeder cattle, this was probably where they'd be brought. But from what she'd learned, it was subordinates who dealt with the logistics of the transporting of feeder cattle, not the bosses.

She wanted badly to see him, to tell him how big an impact he'd had on her life with his pep talk that night she'd gone to the bar. Her horizons had enlarged, and she was independent for the first time in her life. She'd gone from frightened girl to confident woman in a very short time, and she wanted to thank him. She'd almost asked Abby a dozen times if she knew anyone named Donavan, but Abby would hardly travel in those circles. The Ballengers were high society now, even if they weren't social types. They wouldn't hang out in country bars with men who treed them.

Her uncle had tried to get her to come back to his house when word got out that she was working for a living, but she'd stood firm. No, she told Uncle Henry firmly. She wasn't going to be at his mercy until she inherited. And, she added, Mr. Holman was going to expect an accounting in the near future. Her uncle had looked very uncomfortable when she'd said that and she'd called Barry Holman the next morning to ask about her uncle's authority to act on her behalf.

His reply was that her uncle's power of attorney was a very limited one, and it was doubtful that he could do much damage in the short time he had left. Fay wondered about that. Her uncle was shrewd and underhanded. Heaven knew what wheeling and dealing he might have done already without her knowledge.

Pressure of work caught her attention and held it until the early afternoon. She took long enough to eat lunch at a nearby seafood place and came back just in time to catch the tail end of a heated argument coming from Calhoun's office.

"You're being unreasonable, J.D., and you know it!" Calhoun's deep voice carried down the hall.

"Unreasonable, hell," an equally deep voice drawled. "You and I may never see eye to eye on production methods, but while you're feeding out my cattle, you'll do it my way."

"For God's sake, you'd have me out there feeding the damned things with a fork!"

"Not at all. I only want them treated humanely."

"They *are* treated humanely!"

"I wouldn't call an electric cattle prod that. And stressed animals aren't healthy animals."

"Have you ever thought about joining an animal rights lobby?" came the exasperated reply.

"I belong to two, thanks."

The door opened and Fay couldn't drag her eyes away from it. That curt voice was so familiar...

Sure enough, the tall, lithe man who came out of the office in front of Calhoun was equally familiar. Fay couldn't help the radiance of her face, the softness of her eyes as they adored his lean, dark face under the wide brim of his hat.

Donavan. She could have danced on her desk.

But when he turned and saw her, he frowned. His silvery eyes narrowed, glittered. He paused by her desk, his head cocked slightly to one side, a lit cigar dangling from his fingers.

"What are you doing here?" he asked her bluntly.

"I'm filling in for Nita," she began.

"Don't tell me you have to work for a living now, debutante?" he asked in a mocking tone.

She hesitated. He sounded as if he disliked her. But she knew he'd enjoyed the fiesta as much as she had. His behavior puzzled her, intimidated her.

"Well, yes," she stammered. "I do." And she did. For the time being.

"What a hell of a comedown," he murmured with patent disbelief. "Still driving the Mercedes?"

"You know each other?" Calhoun asked narrowly.

Donavan lifted the cigar to his mouth and blew out thick smoke. "Vaguely." He glanced at Calhoun until the other man sighed angrily and went back to his office with a muttered goodbye.

"You've been driving by the bar fairly regularly," he remarked curtly, and she blushed because she couldn't deny it. She'd been looking for him, hoping to have a chance to tell him how he'd helped her turn her life around. But he seemed to be putting a totally different connotation on her actions. "Is that where you found out I did business with the Ballengers?" He didn't even give her time to deny it. "Well, no go, honey. I told you that night, no bored debutante is going to try to make a minor amusement out of me. So if you came here hoping for another shot at me, you might as well quit right now and go home to your caviar and champagne. You're not hard on the eyes, but I'm off the market, is that clear?''

She stared at him in quiet confusion. ''Mr. Holman told me about the job,'' she said with what dignity she had left. ''I don't have a dime until my twenty-first birthday, and I'm living on my own so I have to pay rent. This was the only job available.'' She dropped her gaze to her computer. ''I drove by the bar a time or two, yes. I wanted to tell you that you'd changed my life, that I was learning to stand on my own feet. I wanted to thank you.''

His jaw tautened and he looked more dangerous than ever. ''I don't want thanks, teenage adulation, hero worship or misplaced lust. But you're welcome, if it matters.''

He sounded cynical and mocking. Fay felt chastised. She'd only been grateful, but he made her feel stupid. Maybe she was. She'd spun a few midnight dreams about him. Except for some very innocent dates with boys, she'd never had much attention from the opposite sex. His protective attitude that night in the bar, his quiet handling of what could have become a bad incident, had made her feel feminine and hungry for more of his company. He was telling her that she'd made too much of it, that she was offering him affection that he didn't want or need. It was probably a kindness, but it hurt all the same.

She forced a smile. "You needn't worry. I wasn't planning to follow you around with a wedding band on a hook or anything. I just wanted to thank you for what you did."

"You've done that. So?"

"I . . . have a lot of work to get through. I'm only temporary," she added quickly. "Just until Nita comes back. When I get my legacy, I'll be on the first plane back to Georgia. Honest."

His dark eyebrows plunged above the straight bridge of his nose. "I don't remember asking for any explanations."

"Excuse me, then." She turned her attention back to her keyboard; her hands were cold and numb. She forced them to work. She didn't look up, either. He'd made her feel like what came out of a sausage grinder.

He didn't reply. He didn't linger, either. His measured footsteps went out the door immediately, leaving the pungent scent of cigar smoke in their wake.

Calhoun came back out five minutes later, checking his watch. "I have to be out of the office for an hour or so. Tell Justin when he comes back, will you?"

"Yes, sir," she said, smiling.

He hesitated, his narrowed eyes registering the hurt on her face that she couldn't hide. "Listen, Fay, don't let him upset you," he added quietly. "He doesn't really mean things as personally as they sound, but he rubs everybody the wrong way except Justin.''

"He saved me from a bad situation," she began. "I only wanted to thank him, but he seemed to think I had designs on him or something. My goodness, he thought I came to work here because he did business with you!''

He laughed. "Can't blame him. Several have, and no, I'm not kidding. The more he snarls, the harder some women chase him. He's a catch, too. He makes good money with Mesa Blanco, and his own ranch is nothing to laugh at.''

"Mesa...Blanco?" she stammered, as puzzle pieces began to make a pattern in her mind.

"Sure. Didn't he introduce himself before?" He smiled ruefully. "I guess not. Well, that was J. D. Langley.''

Chapter Three

Fay got through the rest of the day without showing too much of her heartache. She'd had hopes that Donavan might have felt something for her, but he'd dashed those very efficiently. He couldn't have made it more obvious that he wanted no part of her or her monied background. He wouldn't believe that she had to work. Well, of course, she didn't, really. But he might have given her the benefit of the doubt.

It hadn't been a terrible shock to learn that he was J. D. Langley. He did live down to his publicity. Later, she'd found out that Donavan was his middle name and what he was called locally, except by people who did business with him. She certainly understood why the Ballengers hated to see him coming.

She was sorry about his hostility, because the first time she'd ever seen him, there had been a tenderness between them that she'd never experienced. It must have all been on one side, though, she decided miserably.

Well, she told herself as she lay trying to sleep that night, she'd do better to stop brooding and concentrate on her own problems. She had enough, without adding the formidable Mr. Langley to them.

But fate was conspiring against her. The next day, she tried a new cafeteria in Jacobsville and came face-to-face with J. D. Langley as she sat down with her tray.

He gave her a glare that would have stopped traffic. He'd obviously just finished his meal. He was draining his coffee cup. Fay turned her chair so that she wasn't looking directly at him and, with unsteady hands, took her food off the tray.

"I told you yesterday," Donavan said at her shoulder, "that I don't like being chased. Didn't you listen?"

The whip of his voice cut. Not only that, it was loud enough to attract attention from other diners in the crowded room.

Fay's face went red as she glanced at him apprehensively, her green eyes huge as they met the fierce silvery glitter of his.

"I didn't know you were going to be here..." she began uneasily.

"No?" he challenged, his smile an insult in itself. "You didn't recognize my car sitting in the parking lot? Give it up, debutante. I don't like bored little rich girls, so stop following me around. Got that?"

He turned and left the cafeteria. Fay was too humiliated by the unwanted attention to enjoy much of her meal. She left quickly and went back to work.

Following him around, indeed, she muttered to herself while she fed data into her computer. She didn't know what kind of car he drove. The only vehicle she'd seen him in was a battered gray pickup truck, had he forgotten? Perhaps he thought she'd seen his car when he'd come to the feedlot, but she hadn't. The more she saw of him the less she liked him, and she'd hardly been hounding him. She certainly wouldn't again, he could bank on that!

Abby came in the next afternoon with an invitation. "Calhoun and I have to go to a charity ball tonight. I know it's spur-of-the-moment, but would you like to come?"

"Will my uncle be there, do you think?" Fay asked.

"I hardly think so." Abby grinned. "Come on. You've been moping around here for two days, it will be good for you. You can ride with us, and there's a very nice man I want to introduce you to when we get there. He's unattached, personable, and rich enough not to mind that you are."

"Uh, Mr. Langley...?"

"I heard what happened in Cole's Café." Abby grimaced. "J.D. doesn't go to charity balls, so you aren't likely to run into him there."

"Thank God. He was so kind to me the night I met him, but he's been terrible to me ever since. I only wanted to thank him. He thinks I have designs on him." She shuddered. "As if I'd ever chased a man in my life...!"

"You're not J.D.'s kind of woman, Fay," the older woman said gently. "Your wealth alone would keep him at bay, without the difference in your ages. J.D.'s in his early thirties, and he doesn't like younger women."

"I don't think he likes *any* women," Fay replied with a sigh. "Especially me. But I wasn't chasing him, honestly!"

"Don't let it worry you."

"You're sure he won't be there tonight?"

"Absolutely positive," Abby assured her.

Prophetic words. Abby and Calhoun picked Fay up at her apartment house, and drove her to the elegant Whitman estate where the charity ball was already in progress. Fay was wearing a long white silk dress with one shoulder bare and her hair in a very elegant braided bun atop her head. She looked young and fragile...and very rich.

They went through the receiving line and Fay moved ahead of Calhoun and Abby to the refreshment table while they spoke to an acquaintance. She bumped into someone and turned to apologize.

"Again?" J. D. Langley asked with a vicious scowl. "My God, do you have radar?"

Fay didn't say a word. She turned and went back toward Abby and Calhoun, her heart pounding in her chest.

Abby spotted J.D. and grimaced. "I didn't know," she told a shattered Fay. "I swear I didn't. Here, you stick close to us. He won't bother you. Come on, I'll introduce you to Bart and that will solve all your problems. I'm sorry, Fay."

"It wasn't your fault. It's fate, I guess," she said dryly, although her eyes were troubled.

"Arrogant beast," Abby muttered, sparing the tall, elegant man in the dinner jacket a speaking glance. "If he were a little less conceited, you wouldn't have this problem." She drew Fay forward. "Here he is. Bart!"

A thin, lazy looking man with wavy blond hair and mischievous blue eyes turned as his name was called. He greeted Abby warmly and glanced at Fay with open curiosity and delight.

"Well, well, Greek goddesses are back in style again, I see. Do favor me with a waltz before you set off for Mount Olympus, fair damsel."

"This is our newest employee, Fay York," she introduced them. "Fay, this is Bartlett Markham. He's president of the local cattlemen's association."

"Nice to meet you," she said, extending a hand. "Do you know cattle?"

"I grew up on a ranch. I work for a firm of accountants now, but my family still has a pretty formidable Santa Gertrudis purebred operation."

"I don't know much, but I'm learning every day," Fay laughed.

"I'll leave her with you, Bart," Abby said. "Do keep her away from J.D., will you? He seems to think she's stalking him."

"Do tell?" His eyebrows levered up and he grinned. "Why not stalk me instead? I'm a much better catch than J.D., and you won't need preventive shots if you go out with me, either."

Insinuating that she would with J.D., she thought. Rabies probably, she mused venomously, in case he bit her. She smiled at Bart, feeling happier already.

"Consider yourself on the endangered species list, then," she said.

He laughed. "Gladly." He glanced toward the band. "Would you like to dance?"

"Charmed." She gave him her hand and let him lead her to the dance floor, where a live band was playing a bluesy two-step. She knew exactly where J. D. Langley was, as if she really did have radar, so she was careful not to look in that direction.

He noticed. It was impossible not to, when she was dancing with one of his bitterest enemies. He stood quietly against a wall, his silver eyes steady and unblinking as he registered the fluid grace with which she followed her partner's steps. He didn't like the way Markham was holding her, or the way she was responding.

Not that he wanted her, he assured himself. She was nothing but another troublesome woman. A debutante, at that, and over ten years his junior. He had no use for her at all, and he'd made sure she knew it. Their one evening together had sent him tearing away in the opposite direction. She appealed to him terribly. He couldn't afford an involvement with a society girl. He knew he was better off alone, so keeping this tempting little morsel away from him became imperative. If he had to savage her to do it, it was still the best thing for both of them. She was much too soft and delicate for a man like himself. He'd break her spirit and her heart, because he had nothing to give. And his father's reputation in the community made it impossible for him to be seen in public with her in any congenial way. He'd accused her of stalking him, but gossip would have it the other way around. Another money-crazy Langley, critics would scoff, out to snare himself a rich wife. He groaned at just the thought.

He didn't like seeing her with Markham, but there was nothing he could do about it. He shouldn't have come tonight.

He turned away to the refreshment table and poured himself a glass of Scotch.

"You aren't really after Donavan, are you?" Bart asked humorously.

"He flatters himself," she said haughtily.

"That's what I thought. Like father, like son," he said unpleasantly.

"I don't understand."

He made a graceful turn, carrying her with him as the music's tempo increased. "After Donavan's mother died, Rand Langley got into a financial tangle and was about to lose his ranch. My aunt was very young then, plain and shy, but she was filthy rich and single, so Rand set his cap for her. He kept after her until he seduced her, so that she had to marry him or disgrace her family. She was crazy about him. Worshiped the ground he walked on. Then, inevitably, she found out why he really married her and she couldn't live with it. She killed herself."

Fay grimaced. "I'm sorry."

"So were all of us," he added coldly, glaring at J. D. Langley's back. "Rand didn't even come to the funeral. He was too busy spending her money. He died a few years later, and believe me, none of us grieved for him."

"That wasn't Donavan's fault," she felt bound to point out.

"Blood will tell," came the unbelieving reply. "You're well-to-do."

"Yes, but he can't stand me," she replied.

"I don't believe that. I can't imagine J.D. passing up a rich woman."

"How many has he dated over the years?" she asked with faint irritation.

"I don't keep up with his love life," he said tersely, and all his prejudices showed quite clearly. Fay could see that he wouldn't believe a kind word about J. D. Langley if he had proof.

"The two of you don't get along, I gather."

"We disagree on just about everything. Especially on his ridiculous theories about cattle raising," he added sarcastically. "No. We don't get along."

She was quiet after that. Now she understood the situation. It couldn't have been made clearer.

She danced with several eligible bachelors and several married men before the evening ended. It surprised her that J. D. Langley was still present. He remained on the fringes of the dance floor, talking to other men. He asked no one to dance. Fay was sadly certain that he wouldn't ask her.

But in that, she was surprised. The band was playing a soft love song and she watched Bart glance in her direction. But before he could get across the room, Donavan suddenly swung her into his arms and onto the dance floor.

Her heart skipped wildly as she felt the firm clasp of his hand on her waist, his fingers steely as they linked her own.

"This is not a good idea," she said firmly. "I'll think you're encouraging me."

"Not likely. By now Bart's filled you in, hasn't he?" he replied with a mocking smile.

She averted her eyes to the white ruffled shirt he wore under his dinner jacket. On another man it might look effeminate. On Donavan, it looked masculine and very sexy, emphasizing his dark good looks. "I got an earful, thanks," she replied.

He shook her gently. "Stiff as a board," he mused, looking down at her. "Are you afraid to let your guard down? There's very little I could do to you on a dance floor in front of half of Jacobsville."

"You've made your opinion of me crystal clear, Mr. Langley," she said without looking up. "I haven't been stalking you, as you put it, but you're free to think what you like. Do try to remember that I didn't ask you to dance."

"That was the whole purpose of the exercise," he said carelessly. "To make sure you didn't set your cap for me."

"Then why are you dancing with me?"

His lean arm whipped her close on a turn, but he didn't let her go afterward. His dark face was all too close, so that she could smell his tangy after-shave, and his silver eyes bit into hers at point-blank range. "Don't you know?" he asked at her lips.

Her heart tripped as she felt his breath. "Oh, I see," she said suddenly. "You're trying to irritate Bart."

He lifted his head and one eyebrow quirked. "Is that it?"

"What else?" she asked with a nervous laugh, averting her eyes to a fuming Bart nearby. "Listen, I'm not going to be used for any vendettas, by you or your hissing kin."

His fingers curled into hers and drew them to his broad chest. It rose and fell heavily, and he stared over her dark head without seeing anything. "I don't have any vendettas," he said quietly. "But I won't be accused of following in my father's footsteps."

She could feel the pain in those terse words, but she didn't remark on it. Her eyes closed and she drank in the delicious masculine scent of him. "I won't be rich for another week or two," she murmured. "Until the legal work goes through, I'm just a temporary secretary."

He laughed in spite of himself. "I see. For two weeks you're on my level. No Mercedes. No mansion. No padded checkbook."

"Something like that." She sighed and snuggled closer. "How about a wild, passionate affair? We could throw the coats on the closet floor and you could have your way with me under somebody's silver fox stole."

He burst out laughing. His steely arm drew her close as he made a sudden turn, and her body throbbed with the sensations it caused in her untried body.

"Hasn't anyone told you yet that I belong to two animal rights groups?"

"So you're one of those people who protest lab animal experiments that save little children's lives and throw paint on people who wear fur coats?" she asked, her temper rising.

"Not me. I'm no fanatic. I just think animals have the right to humane treatment, even in medical facilities." His arm tightened. "As for throwing paint on fur coats, a few lawsuits should stem that habit. The idea is to stop further slaughter of wild animals. A fur coat is already a dead animal."

She shivered. "You make it sound morbid."

One silver eye narrowed. "Do you wear fur?"

She chuckled. "I can't. Fur makes me break out in hives."

He began to smile. "A rich girl with no furs. What a tragedy."

"I have plenty of velvet coats, thanks very much. I think they're much more elegant than fur and they don't shed." She moved closer, shocked when his hand caught her hip and contracted painfully. "Ouch!" she protested.

He moved her back an inch. "Don't push your luck," he said, his voice low and faintly threatening, like his glittery eyes. "You're pretty sexy in that little number you're wearing, and I'm easily aroused. Want me to prove it?"

"No, thanks," she said quickly. "I'll take your word for it."

He laughed as he spun her around in a neat turn. "For a sophisticated debutante, sometimes you're a contradiction. Is that a blush?"

"It's hot in here."

"Ah. The conventional excuse." He leaned close and brushed his cheek against hers. "Too bad you're rich."

"Is it? Why?" she asked in a tone that sounded, unfortunately, all too breathless.

He nibbled gently on her earlobe. "Because I'm dynamite in bed."

"Do tell?" She hid her face against him. "Are you?" she whispered shakily.

His lean hand slid up her back and into the coiled hair at her nape. He caressed it gently while he held her, the music washing over them in a sultry silence.

"So I've been told." His chin rubbed softly against her temple, his breath coming roughly. "But why take someone else's word for it?"

She forced a laugh. "Isn't this a little sudden? I mean, just a day ago you were giving me hell for eating lunch in the same restaurant with you."

"I'm sure Bart told you the problem. Rich, you're right off my Christmas list. Poor, you're an endangered species." His hand contracted, coaxing her face up to his glittery eyes.

"Should I cut and run?" she asked, her voice husky.

"Do you really want to?" he whispered.

As he spoke, he moved closer, and his powerful thighs brushed hers. Even through all the layers of fabric, she felt the imprint of them, the strength. His hand slid down her back to her waist and pulled, very gently, so that she was pressed right up to him, welded from breast to thigh. He watched her eyes and something masculine and arrogant kindled in his gaze as he felt the faint shiver of her soft body.

"Do you like Chinese food?" he asked.

She nodded.

"I like to drive up to Houston for it. There's a good restaurant just inside the city limits. How about it?"

Her heart jumped. "Are you asking me out?"

"Sounds like it," he mused. "Don't expect steak and lobster. I make a good salary, but it doesn't run to champagne."

She colored furiously. "Please, don't," she said quickly. "I'm not like that."

He touched her face gently. "Yes, I know. It makes it harder. Do you think I enjoyed hurting you?" he asked harshly, and for an instant something showed in his eyes that startled her. He looked away. "There's no future for us, little one."

She felt him hesitating. Any second, he was going to take back that supper invitation.

"Just Chinese food," she prompted, one slender hand poking him gently in the ribs.

He started, and she grinned at him. "And no moonlight seduction on the way home," she added. "As you said, it isn't wise to start things we can't finish."

"I could finish that," he murmured dryly.

She cleared her throat. "Well, I don't take chances. I'll risk my stomach with you, but not my heart."

He cocked an eyebrow. "Does that mean that making love with me might enslave you?" he teased.

"Exactly. Besides, I never sleep with a man on the first date."

There was the faintest movement of his eyelashes. He averted his gaze to a point beyond her head. He couldn't admit that it bothered him, thinking of her with other men. She was a debutante and filthy rich, surely there had been a steady stream of suitors. She might have more experience even than he did. He'd never thought about a woman's past before. It had never occurred to him to wonder how experienced his lover of the evening actually was. But with Fay, he wondered.

"What's wrong?" she asked curiously.

He glanced down at her. She looked very innocent until she smiled, and then her eyes crinkled and there was a sophistication in them that made him feel cool. "Nothing."

"That's usually the woman's line, isn't it?"

"Equal rights," he reminded her. "Friday night. I'll pick you up at six."

"I don't live with Uncle Henry anymore," she began.

"I know where you live," he replied. "We'll eat Chinese food and you can show me what you know. It should be quite an experience . . ."

Long after the dance was over and she was back in her apartment, she worried over that last statement. She felt as if she were about to get in well over her head.

She wanted Donavan more than she'd ever wanted anything in her life. A date with him was the gold at the end of the rainbow. But she'd pretended to be something she wasn't, and she didn't know what she was going to do if he took her up on it.

Abby noticed Fay's preoccupation the next day when she stopped by to see Calhoun.

"You're positively morose!" Abby exclaimed. "What's wrong?"

"Donavan asked me out."

Her eyebrows went up. "J.D. asked you out? But he hates rich women."

"Yes, I know. I told him I was going to be poor for two more weeks, so I guess he thought it was safe enough until my inheritance comes through."

"I see." Abby didn't say anything, but she began to look worried herself. "Fay, I never thought to mention it, because J.D. was giving you such a hard time, but he's something of a womanizer..."

"I figured that out for myself," she murmured with a smile. "It shows."

"He's a gentleman, in his way. Just don't give him too much rope. He'll hang you with it."

"I know that, too. I'll be careful."

Abby hesitated. "If it helps, I know how you feel. I was crazy about Calhoun, but he liked a different kind of woman altogether. We had a very rocky path to the altar."

"He's crazy about you, though. Anyone can see that."

Abby smiled contentedly. "Of course he is. But it wasn't always that way."

"Donavan already said that he doesn't want commitment. I'm not going to get my hopes up. But an evening out with him... Well, it's going to be like brushing heaven, you know?"

"I do, indeed." Abby smiled, remembering her first date with Calhoun. She glanced back at Fay, her eyes wistful. She only hoped their newest employee wasn't going to be badly hurt. Everyone locally knew that J. D. Langley wasn't a marrying man. But Abby would have bet her prize bull that Fay was as innocent as Abby herself had once been. If she was, she had a lot of heartache in store. When J.D. found out, and he would, he'd drop Fay like a hot rock. Innocents were not his style.

* * *

Fay went through the motions of working like a zombie for the next week, with a dull and tedious weekend in between that did little for her nerves. Donavan didn't come by the feedlot at all, and when she left the office the next Friday afternoon, she still hadn't heard from him. For all she knew, he might have forgotten all about her.

The phone was ringing even as she got in the door, and she grabbed up the receiver as if it were a life preserver.

"Hello?" she said breathlessly.

"I'll be by in an hour. You hadn't forgotten?" Donavan drawled.

"How could I?" she asked, adding mischievously, "I love Chinese food."

He chuckled. "That puts me in my place, I guess. See you."

He hung up and Fay ran to dress. The only thing in her closet that would suit a fairly casual evening out was a pale green silk suit and she hated wearing it. It screamed big money, something sure to set Donavan's teeth on edge. But other than designer jeans and a silk blouse, or evening gowns, it was all she had. The cotton pantsuit she'd worn to work today was just too wrinkled and stained to wear out tonight. It wouldn't have been suitable anyway.

She teamed the silk suit with a nice cotton blouse and sat down to wait, after renewing her makeup. She only hoped that he wasn't going to take one look at her and run. If he didn't throw her over entirely, she was going to have to invest in some medium-priced clothing!

Chapter Four

Just as Fay had feared, Donavan's first glimpse of her silk suit brought a scowl to his face.

"It's old," she said inadequately, and looked miserable. She locked her fingers together and stared at him with sadness all over her face.

He shoved his hands into the pockets of his gray slacks. He was wearing a white cotton shirt and a blue blazer with them, a black Stetson cocked over one eye and matching boots on his feet. He looked nice, but hardly elegant or wealthy. Her silk suit seemed to point out all the differences between the life-style she was used to, and his own.

"You look very nice," he said quietly.

"And very expensive," she added on a curt laugh. "I'm sorry."

"Why?"

"I didn't want you to think I wore this on purpose," she said, faltering.

He lifted an eyebrow and smiled mockingly. "I'm taking you out for a Chinese dinner. A proposal of marriage doesn't come with the egg roll."

She blushed furiously. "I know that."

"Then why bother about appearances?" He shrugged. "A date is one thing. A serious relationship is something else." His silver eyes narrowed. "Let's settle that at the outset. I have nothing serious or permanent in mind. Even if we wind up as the hottest couple in town between the sheets, there still won't be anything offered in the way of commitment."

"I knew that already," she said, steeling herself not to react to the provocative statement.

"Good." He glanced around the apartment, frowning slightly. "This is pretty spartan, isn't it?" he asked, suddenly realizing how frugally she seemed to be living.

"It's all I could afford on my salary," she told him. She wrapped her arms across her breasts and smiled. "I don't mind it. It's just a place to sleep."

"Henry doesn't help you financially?" he persisted.

"He can't," she explained. "He's got his own financial woes. I'll be fine when he turns over my affairs to Mr. Holman and I can get to my trust."

Donavan didn't say a word, but suddenly he was beginning to see things she apparently didn't. If Henry was having money problems, surely his control of Fay's estate would give him the means of solving them, even if he had to pay her back later. The fact that he was suffering a reversal didn't bode well for Fay, but she seemed oblivious. Perhaps like most rich women she didn't know or care much about handling money.

He was aware that he'd been silent a long time. He took his hands out of his pockets and caught her slender fingers in his. They were cold, like ice. "We'd better go," he said, drawing her along with him.

Fay had never realized how exciting it could be to hold hands with a man. He linked her fingers into his as they walked, and she felt the sensuous contraction all the way to her toes. It was like walking on a cloud, she thought. She could almost float.

Donavan was feeling something similar and fighting it tooth and nail. He hadn't really wanted this date at all, but something stronger than his will had forced him into it. Fay was a delicious little morsel, full of contradictions. He'd always liked puzzles. She was one he really wanted to solve, even if his inclination was to get her into the nearest bed with all possible haste.

She had to be experienced. She'd never denied that. He wondered if pampered rich boys were as anemic in bed as they seemed when he saw them at board meetings. His contempt for the upper classes was, he knew, a result of his father's ruthless greed.

He could still barely believe the whole episode, his father running pell-mell after a woman half his age when his wife of twenty years was just barely in her grave. It had disgusted and shocked him, and led to a confrontation of stellar proportions. He hadn't spoken to his father afterward, and his presence at his father's funeral two years later was only a nod to convention. It wasn't until much later that he'd learned why Rand Langley had been so ruthless. It had been to save the family ranch, which had been Langley land for three generations. Not that it excused what he'd done, but it did at least explain it. Rand had wanted Donavan to inherit the ranch. Marrying money had been the only way he could keep it.

"You're very quiet," Fay remarked on the way to Houston. "Are you sorry you asked me out?"

He glanced at her. "No. I was remembering."

"Yes?"

He was smoking one of the small cigars he favored, his gray eyes thoughtful as they lingered on the long road ahead. "My father disgraced himself to marry money, to keep the ranch for me and my children, if I ever have any. Ironic, that I've never married and never want to, because of him."

She folded her hands primly in her lap. It flattered her that he was willing to tell her something so personal.

"If you don't have children, what will happen to your ranch?" she asked.

"I've got a ten-year-old nephew," he said. "My sister's boy. His father's been dead for years. My sister remarried three years ago, and she died last year. Her husband got custody. But he's just remarried, and last month he stuck Jeffrey in a military school. The boy's in trouble constantly, and he hates his stepfather." He took a long draw from the cigar, scowling. "That's why I was sitting in that bar the night you walked in. I was trying to decide what to do. Jeff wants to come out here and live with me."

"Can't he?"

He shook his head. "No chance. His father and I don't get along. He'd more than likely refuse just to get at me. His new wife is pregnant and he doesn't seem to care about Jeff at all."

"That's sad," she said. "Does he miss his mother?"

"He never talks about her."

"Probably because he cares too much," she said. "I miss my parents," she added unexpectedly. "They died in a plane crash. Even if I never saw much of them, they were still my parents."

"What do you mean, you never saw much of them?"

She laughed softly. "They liked traveling. I was in school, and they didn't want to interrupt my education. I stayed at home with an elderly great-aunt. She liked me very much, but it was kind of lonely. Especially during holidays." She stared out the window, aware of his curious stare. "If I ever have kids, I'll be where they are," she said suddenly. "And they won't ever have to spend Christmas without me."

"I suppose," he began slowly, "there are some things money won't buy."

"An endless list," she agreed. "Beginning and ending with love."

He chuckled softly, to lighten the atmosphere. He glanced sideways at her. "Money can buy love, you know," he murmured.

"Well, not really," she disagreed. "It can buy the illusion of it, but I wouldn't call a timed session in bed 'love.'"

He burst out laughing. "No," he said after a minute. "I don't suppose it is. They say that type of experience is less than satisfying. I wouldn't know. I couldn't find any pleasure in a body I had to pay for."

"I can understand that."

There was a pleasant tension in the silence that dropped between them. Minutes later, Donavan pulled up in front of a Chinese restaurant and cut off the engine.

"This is it," he said. He helped her out of the car and escorted her inside.

It was a very nice restaurant, with Chinese music playing softly in the background and excellent service.

Donavan watched her covertly as he sampled the jasmine tea the waitress had served. "Tell me about your job. How does it feel to work for a living?"

Her eyes brightened and she smiled. "I like it very much," she confessed. "I've never been responsible for my own life before. I've always had people telling me what to do and how to do it. The night I met you at the bar really opened my eyes. You made me see what my life was like, showed me that I could change it if I wanted to. I wasn't kidding when I said you turned my world around."

"I thought the job was a means to an end," he confessed, smiling at his own folly. "I've been chased before, and by well-to-do women who saw me as a challenge."

"You're not bad looking," she said demurely, averting her eyes. "And you're very much a man. But I meant it when I said I wasn't chasing you. I have too much pride to behave that way."

Probably she did. He liked her honesty. He liked the way she looked and dressed, too. She wasn't beautiful, but she was elegant and well-mannered, and she had a big heart. He found himself wondering how Jeff would react to her.

They ate in a pleasant silence and talked about politics and the weather, everything except themselves. All too soon it was time to start back for Jacobsville.

"How are you and your uncle getting along?" Donavan asked on the way back.

"We speak and not much more. Uncle Henry's worried about something," she added. "He gets more nervous by the day."

He'd never thought of her uncle as a nervous man. Perhaps it had something to do with Fay's inheritance.

"Suppose you inherit only a few dollars and an apology?" he asked suddenly.

She laughed. "That isn't likely."

"But if it was?"

She thought about it seriously. "It would be hard," she confessed. "I'm not used to asking the price of anything, or denying myself a whim purchase. But like anything else, I expect I could get used to it. I don't mind hard work."

He nodded. That would make her life easier.

He turned off onto a farm road just at the outskirts of Jacobsville.

"Where are we going?" she asked, glancing around at unfamiliar terrain.

"I'm going to show you my ranch," he said simply. His eyes lanced over her and he smiled wickedly. "Then I'm going to shove you into the henhouse and have my way with you."

"Do you have a henhouse?" she asked excitedly.

"Yes. And a flock of chickens to go with it. I like fresh eggs."

He didn't add that he often had to budget in between cattle sales, even on the good salary he made.

"I guess you have your own beef, too?" she asked.

"Not for slaughter," he replied. "I like animals too much to raise one to kill. Mesa Blanco has slaughter cattle, but I don't spend any more time around them than I have to."

The picture she was getting of him didn't have a lot to do with the image he projected. An animal lover with a core of steel was unusual.

"Do you have dogs and cats?"

He smiled slowly. "And puppies and kittens," he said. "I give them away when the population gets out of control, and most of mine are neutered. It's criminal to turn an unneutered animal loose on the streets." He slowed as the road curved toward a simple white frame house. "Ever had a dog or cat of your own?"

"No," she said sadly. "My parents weren't animal lovers. My mother would have fainted at the thought of cat hair on her Louis Quinze furniture."

"I'd rather have the cat than the furniture," he remarked.

She smiled. "So would I."

His heart lifted. She wasn't at all what he'd expected. He pulled up in front of the ranch house and cut off the engine.

There were flowers everywhere, from shrubs to trees to beds of them right and left around the porch. She could see them by the fierce light of the almost-full moon. "How beautiful!" she exclaimed.

"Thank you."

"You planted them?"

"Nobody else. I like flowers," he said defensively as he got out and helped her out of the car.

"I didn't say a word," she assured him. "I like flowers, too."

He unlocked the front door while she glanced covetously along the long front porch at the old-fashioned swing and rocking chair. Somewhere nearby cattle made pleasant mooing noises.

"Do you keep a lot of cattle here?" she asked.

"I have purebred Santa Gertrudis," he told her. "Stud cattle, not beef cattle."

"Why doesn't that surprise me?" she teased.

He laughed, standing aside to let her enter the house.

The living room was done in Early American, and it looked both neat and lived-in. For a bachelor, he was a good housekeeper. She said so.

"Thanks, but I can't take all the credit. My foreman's wife looks after things when I can't."

She was insanely jealous of the foreman's wife, all at once.

He saw her expression and smiled. "She's fifty and happily married."

She blushed, moving farther into the room.

"Look out," he warned.

Before the words went silent, her foot was attacked by a tiny ball of fur with teeth.

"Good heavens!" she exclaimed, laughing. "A miniature tiger!" she kidded.

"I'm training her to be an attack cat. I call her Bee."

"Bee?"

He grinned. "Short for Beelzebub. You can't imagine what she did to the curtains a day or so ago."

She reached down and picked up the tiny thing. It looked up at her with a calico face and the softest, most loving blue-green eyes she'd ever seen, with black fur outlining them.

"Why, she's beautiful!" she exclaimed.

"I think so."

The kitten's eyes half closed as it began to purr and knead her jacket with its tiny paws.

"She'll pick that silk," he said, reaching for the kitten.

She looked at him curiously. "That doesn't matter," she said, surprised by his comment.

His silver eyes registered his own surprise as they looked deeply into hers. "That suit must have cost a small fortune," he persisted. He extricated the kitten, despite her protests, and carried it into the bedroom, closing the door behind him.

"Want some coffee?" he asked.

"That would be nice."

"It will only take a minute or so." He tossed his hat onto the hat rack and went into the kitchen.

Fay wandered around the living room, stopping at a photograph on the mantel. It was of a young boy, a studio pose. He looked a lot like Donavan, except that his eyes were dark, and he had a more rounded face. He looked sad.

"That's Jeff," he told her from the doorway. He leaned against it, waiting for the coffee to brew. His long legs were crossed, like his arms, and he looked very masculine and sexy with his jacket off and the top buttons of his shirt unfastened over a thicket of jet black hair.

"He favors you," she remarked. "Did your sister look like you?"

"Quite a lot," he said. "But her eyes were darker than mine. Jeff has his father's eyes."

"What does he like?" she asked. "I mean, is he a sports fan?"

"He doesn't care much for football. He likes martial arts, and he's good at them. He's a blue belt in tae kwon do—a Korean martial art that concentrates on kicking styles."

"Isn't that a demonstration sport in the summer Olympics?"

He smiled, surprised. "Yes, it is. Jeff hopes to be able to participate in the 1996 summer games in Atlanta."

"A group of Atlantans worked very hard to get the games to come there," she recalled. "One of my friends worked in the archives at Georgia Tech—a lot of the people on campus were active in that committee."

"You don't have many friends here, do you?" he asked.

"Abby Ballenger is a friend," she corrected. "And I get along well with the girls at the office."

"I meant friends in your own social class."

She put the picture of Jeff back on the mantel. "I never had friends in my own social class. I don't like their idea of fun."

"Don't you?"

He moved closer. His hands slid around her waist from behind and tugged her against him. His cheek nuzzled hers roughly. "What was their idea of fun?"

"Sleeping around," she said huskily. "That's... suicidal these days. All it takes is the wrong partner and you can die."

"I know." His lips slid down her long, elegant neck. His tongue tip found the artery at her throat and pressed there, feeling it accelerate wildly at his touch. His fingers slid to her slender hips and dug in, welding her to his hard thighs.

"Donavan?" she whispered unsteadily.

His hands flattened on her stomach, making odd little motions that sent tremors down her long legs and a rush of warmth into her bloodstream.

She didn't act very experienced. The camouflage was only good at long range, he thought as he drank in the gardenia scent of her skin. He should have been disappointed, because he'd wanted her badly tonight. But something inside him was elated at his growing suspicion that she was innocent. He had to find out if it was true.

"Turn your mouth up for me, Fay," he whispered at her chin. "I want to taste it under my own."

The words sent thrills down to her toes and curled them. Blind, deaf, she raised her face and turned it, feeling the sudden warm pressure of his mouth on her parted lips.

It wasn't at all what he'd expected. The contact was explosive. He'd been in complete control until he touched her. Now, suddenly he was fighting to keep his head at all. He turned her in his arms and caught his breath as he felt her body melt hungrily into his.

It shouldn't have happened like this. He could barely think. His hands bit into the backs of her thighs and lifted her, pulled at her, needing the close contact as he'd never needed anything. His legs began to tremble as his body went taut and capable, and his hands became ruthless.

Fay moaned. Never at any time in her life had she felt such a sudden, vicious fever of longing. She could always pull back, until now. With a tiny gasp, she lifted her arms around his neck and gave in completely. She felt him against her stomach, knew that he was already painfully aroused. She couldn't manage enough willpower to deny him, whatever the cost, whatever the risk. He was giving her a kind of pleasure she'd never dreamed of experiencing.

He invaded the silk jacket and the blouse she wore under it. He unbuttoned them and drew the fabric aside seconds before his mouth went down against the bare curve of her breast above her lacy bra. She'd never been touched like that. She clung to him, shivering as his lips became ruthless, his face rubbing the bra strap aside so he could nuzzle down far enough to find the hard, warm nipple.

She cried out. It was beyond bearing, sensation upon hot sensation, anguished joy. Her fingers tangled in his thick, dark hair and pulled at it as he suckled her in a silence throbbing with need.

"You taste of gardenias," he breathed urgently. "Soft and sweet . . . Fay . . . !"

His hands were as urgent as his voice. He unfastened her bra and slid it, along with her half-unbuttoned jacket and blouse, right down to her waist. His glazed eyes lingered for one long minute on the uncovered pink and mauve beauty of her naked breasts with their crowns hard and tip-tilted. Then his mouth and his hands were touching them, and she was glorying in his own pleasure, in the sweet delight of his ardor.

"So beautiful," he whispered as he drew his face over her soft breasts. "Fay, you make my body throb. Feel it. Feel me..."

One hand went to gather her hips close to his, to emphasize what he was saying. She moaned and searched blindly for his mouth, inviting a kiss as deep and ardent as the hand enjoying her soft breasts in the stillness of the room.

"Little one," he said huskily, "do you know what's going to happen between us now? Do you want me?"

"Yes!" she whispered achingly, hanging at his lips.

His body shivered with its blatant need. It had never been so urgent before, with any woman. He bit at her mouth. "Do you have anything to use? Are you on the pill?"

She hesitated. "No."

No. The word echoed through his swaying mind. No, she wasn't protected. He could have her, but he could also make her pregnant. Pregnant! He said something explicit and embarrassing, then he put his hands on her upper arms and thrust her away from him. He went blindly toward the kitchen and slammed the door behind him.

Fay sat down on the sofa, fastening hooks and buttons with hands so unsteady that she missed half the buttons and had to start over. It was a long time before she was back in order again, and only a few seconds after that, Donavan came in with a tray of coffee.

She couldn't look at him. She knew her face looked like rice paper. She was still trembling visibly, too, her mouth red and swollen, her breathing erratic and irregular.

He put a cup of black coffee in front of her without saying anything.

She didn't raise her eyes when she felt the sofa depress near her. She reached for the cup, barely able to hold it for the unsteadiness of her icy fingers.

A big, warm hand came to support hers, and when she looked up, his eyes weren't angry at all. They were faintly curious and almost affectionate.

"Thank you," she stammered as she sipped the hot, black liquid.

He smiled. A real smile, not the mocking ones she was used to. "You're welcome."

"I'm so sorry . . . !" she began nervously.

He put a long finger over her soft lips. "No. I am. I shouldn't have let it go so far."

"You were angry," she said hesitantly, her eyes glancing with sheer embarrassment off his before they fell to her cup.

"I was hotter than I've been in years and I had to stop," he said simply, and without anger. "It doesn't put a man in a sparkling mood, let me tell you."

"Oh."

He leaned back and sipped his own coffee, his eyes quiet and faintly acquisitive. "Why are you still a virgin?" he asked suddenly.

The coffee cup made a nosedive, and she only just caught it in time. Her gaze hit his with staggering impact. "What did you say?"

"You heard me," he accused softly. "You can't even put on an act, can you? The second I touch you intimately, you're mine."

She flushed and looked away. "Rub it in," she invited.

"Oh, I intend to," he said with malicious glee. "I'm not sure I've ever made love to a virgin in my life. It was fascinating. You just go right in headfirst, don't you? There's not even a sense of self-preservation in you."

She glared at him. "Having fun?"

"Sure." He rested his arm over the back of the sofa and his gaze was slow and thorough as it fell to her breasts and watched their soft rise and fall. "Pretty little creature," he mused. "All pink and dusk."

"You stop that, J. D. Langley," she muttered hotly. "It isn't decent to even talk about it."

One eyebrow went up. "This is the nineties," he reminded her.

"Wonderful," she told him. "Life is liberal. No more rules and codes of behavior. No wonder the world's a mess."

He leaned back, chuckling. "As it happens, I agree with you. Rules aren't a bad thing, when they prevent the kind of insanity that's gripping the world today. But periodically, people have to find that out for themselves. Ever heard of the Roaring Twenties?" he added.

"Gin flowed like water, women smoked, sexually transmitted diseases ran rampant because everybody was promiscuous..."

"You're getting the idea. But it's nothing new. People had cycles when rules were suspended even back in the Roman Empire. There were orgies and every evil known to man thrived. Then society woke up and the cycle started all over again. The only certain thing in life, Miss York, is change."

"I suppose so. But it's discouraging."

"Maybe you haven't heard, but the majority of people in this country feel exactly the same way you do," he said. "America is still a very moral place, little one. But it's what's different that makes news, not what's traditional."

"I see." She smiled. "That's encouraging."

"You come from wealth. Odd that you don't have an exaggerated sense of morality to go with it."

"You mean, because I was rich, I should be greedy and pleasure-loving and indifferent to my fellow man?" she teased. "Actually, that's a stereotype."

"I get the picture." He stared at her silently, his eyes growing dark with memory. "I wanted you like hell. But in a way, I'm glad you aren't on the pill."

She eyed him curiously. "You didn't sound glad."

"Wanting hurts a man when he can't satisfy it," he explained matter-of-factly. "But you weren't on the pill and I didn't have anything with me to protect you from pregnancy. That's one risk I'll never take."

She smiled at him. "I feel the same way."

His eyes warmed. "We'd better not create any accidental people," he said softly. "That's why I stopped. That," he added, "and the fact that I'm too old-fashioned to dishonor a chaste woman. Go ahead. Laugh," he invited. "But it's how I feel."

"Oh, Donavan, you and I are throwbacks to another time," she said heavily. "There's no place for us on earth."

"Why, sure there is, honey," he disagreed. "I'll carry you to church with me one Sunday and prove to you that we're not alone in the way we think. Listen, it's the radicals who are the minority." He leaned closer. "But the radicals are the ones who make news."

She laughed. "I guess so. I'd like to go to church with you," she said shyly. "I haven't been in a long time. Our housekeeper used to let me go to services with her, but when she quit I had no way to get there. It was before I was old enough to drive."

"Poor little rich girl," he said, but he smiled and the words sounded affectionate.

She smiled back. Everything had changed, suddenly. She looked at him and knew without question that she could love him if she was ever given the chance.

He reached out and tapped her cheek. "Let's go. And from now on, stay out of lonely ranch houses with amorous bachelors. Got that?"

"You were the one who dragged me here," she exclaimed.

"That's right, blame it all on me," he agreed after he'd put the coffee things away and then escorted her out the door. "It's always the man who leads the sweet, innocent girl into a life of sin."

She frowned. "Isn't it the woman who's supposed to lead the innocent man into it?"

He raised both eyebrows as he locked the door. "There aren't any innocent men."

"A likely story. What about priests and monks?"

He sighed. "Well, other than them," he conceded.

"I like your house," she said.

He opened the car door and put her inside. "I like it, too." He got in and started the engine, pausing to glance her way. "We may be heading for a fall, but I'm game if you are."

"Game?" she asked blankly.

He slid a lean hand under her nape and brought her face under his, very gently. He bent to kiss her, with tenderness and respect. "In the old days," he whispered, "they called it courting."

She felt a wave of heat rush over her. Wide-eyed, she stared helplessly up at him.

He nodded, his face solemn. "That's right, I said I didn't believe in marriage. But there's always the one

woman who can make a man change his mind." His
eyes dropped to her mouth. "I want Jeff. If I'm married I have a good chance of getting him. But you and
I could give each other a lot, too. If you're willing,
we'll start spending time together and see where it
leads."

"I'm rich," she began hesitantly.

"Don't worry. I won't hold it against you," he
whispered, smiling as he kissed her again. What he
didn't mention was that he had his own suspicions
about her future. He didn't think she was going to inherit anything at all, and that would put her right in
his league. She'd be lost and alone, except for him,
when the boom fell. She was sweet and biddable and
he wanted her. Jeff needed a stable environment. It
wouldn't hurt his chances with the new president of
Mesa Blanco to be a settled family man, either, but
that was only a minor consideration. Jeff came first.
He'd worry about the complications later. Right now,
he was going to get in over his head for once without
looking too closely at his motives.

Chapter Five

It was all Fay could do to work the next day. She was so lighthearted that she wondered how she managed to keep both feet on the floor.

Her dreams of being with Donavan honestly hadn't included marriage because he'd said that he didn't believe in it. In fact, he'd given her hell for chasing him. How ironic that she'd landed in his orbit at all.

Probably, she had to admit, he needed a wife so that he could gain custody of his nephew, and to help him get ahead in his job. He didn't want a rich wife.

But why, then, was he paying her any attention at all? She'd been honest with him. She'd told him that in a couple of weeks she stood to inherit a fortune. Hadn't he believed her?

Work piled up and she realized that she was paying more attention to her own thoughts than she was to her job, so she settled down to the job-related problems.

"How's everything going?" Abby asked when she came by to meet Calhoun for lunch.

"Great!"

Abby lifted a curious eyebrow. "Really?"

She glanced around her and leaned forward. "Donavan's taking me out."

"J.D.?"

"Don't look so horrified," Fay laughed. "He's serious. He was the perfect gentleman last night and he actually talked about a commitment."

"J.D.?"

Fay nodded. "J.D. Did you know he had a nephew and there's a custody suit in the offing?"

"Yes," Abby said, sobering at once. "The poor little boy's had a hard time. I don't like J.D. a lot, but I'll give him credit for caring about Jeff. He really does." She frowned. "Is that why he's talking seriously?"

"Probably," Fay said, then she smiled. "I don't have any illusions that he's suddenly discovered undying love for me. But he might learn to love me one day. Love takes time."

"Yes," Abby said, remembering. "But you're still rich."

"He said it wouldn't matter."

Abby didn't say another word, until she was alone with Calhoun. "I'm afraid Fay's heading for a bad fall," she told him when they were sharing a quick lunch. "J.D. doesn't seem to mind about her inheritance, but you know how he is about rich women."

"I think he's got some suspicions that her Uncle Henry isn't telling her everything. I have some of my own," he added. "I wonder if Fay has anything left to inherit."

"I had the same feeling. Poor Fay. J.D. doesn't love her, I know he doesn't. He's too much of a womanizer to feel anything deep for a woman."

Calhoun lifted an eyebrow and pursed his lips. "He may be a reforming womanizer." He covered her hand with his and clasped it affectionately. "We all meet our Waterloo eventually. God, I'm glad I met mine with you!"

"Oh, so am I, my darling," she said softly. She leaned forward and kissed him tenderly, despite the amused looks from other diners. "You and the boys are my whole life."

"We've had a good beginning," he agreed. "And the best is still yet to come. We're very lucky."

"Very. I hope Fay fares as well," she added before she concentrated on her food instead of her sexy husband.

Fay didn't see Donavan again for a few days. He'd phoned just to say that he was going out of town on business and that he'd call her when he got back. He hadn't sounded anything like an impatient lover, although he had sounded impatient, as if he hadn't wanted to call her in the first place. She'd been morose ever since, wondering if he'd had second thoughts. Her joy deflated almost at once.

From the day Donavan left, her life went downhill. Two days later she had to go to see Barry Holman about her inheritance. A nervous Uncle Henry was in the office when she got there, and Mr. Holman didn't look very happy.

"Sit down, Fay," Barry said quietly, standing until she was seated.

"It's bad news, isn't it?" she asked, looking from one of them to the other with quick, uneasy eyes.

"I'm afraid so," Barry began, and went on to tell her the bad news. She was penniless.

"I'm sorry, honey," Uncle Henry said heavily. "I did my best, honest to God I did. I pushed you at Sean because I hoped the two of you might hit it off. Sean's rich." His shoulders moved helplessly. "I thought if you married him, you wouldn't have to give up so much."

"Why didn't you tell me?" she asked miserably.

"I didn't know how," he replied. "Your father was a speculator, but for once, he picked the wrong thing to speculate on. I didn't know until a few weeks ago myself, when I tried to liquidate the stock. It fell almost overnight. There's nothing left. Just nothing."

He spread his hands. "Fay, you can always come back and live with me..."

"I have a job," she said thinly, remembering almost at once that it was only a temporary job and would soon end. She felt like crying.

"You still have the Mercedes," Barry said surprisingly. "Your father had the foresight to take out insurance that would pay it off if he died. That's yours, and it has a high resale value. I could handle that for you, if you like. Then you'd have a little ready capital and enough over to buy a smaller car."

"I'd appreciate that," she said dully. "I'll get the papers together and bring them by in the morning, if that's all right."

"That will be fine. There are just a few more details, and I'll need your signature in several places..."

Fay hardly heard anything else that was said. She felt numb. In shock. Just a week ago, she'd been in Donavan's arms with a whole future to look forward to and an inheritance to fall back on. Now she had nothing at all. Even Donavan had seemed to have second thoughts, because he'd certainly dropped her flat.

What if he'd only wanted her for the money in the first place? she thought with hysteria. Or to help him provide a settled home so that he could get custody of his nephew?

The more she worried it in her mind, the worse it got. Donavan hadn't wanted her when she was rich, he'd made sure she knew it. Then all at once, about the time he decided to fight for custody of his nephew, he became suddenly interested in her.

It all fit. The only thing that didn't was his abrupt lack of interest. Had he decided he didn't need her after all? Well, she wouldn't do him much good now, she thought wildly. She was just another member of the working class, and what was she going to do when her job folded?

She went through the motions of her job for the rest of the day, white-faced and terrified. Calhoun noticed, but when he asked what was wrong, she only smiled and pretended it was a headache.

That didn't fool him. He knew too much about women. He picked up the phone and called Barry Holman.

"I know it's all confidential and you can't tell me anything," Calhoun said. "But you can pause in significant places. I only want to help. Fay didn't get a damned thing did she?"

There was a long pause.

"That's what I thought," Calhoun said quietly. "Poor kid."

"She really needs that job," Barry replied. "Knowing it's only temporary is probably eating her up. She's never had to depend on herself before."

"No problem there," Calhoun returned, smiling. "Fay's got a job here as long as she can type. We'll find a niche for her. Damn Henry!"

"Not his fault," Barry said. "A bad investment gone sour, that's all. The old story, but a tragic one for Fay. All she's got left is the Mercedes. And you didn't hear this from me," he added firmly.

"Of course not! I'll just sort of mention that she's working out too well to let go and we want to keep her on."

Barry chuckled. "She'll appreciate that."

"We appreciate her. For a debutante, she's a hell of a hard worker." His eyes narrowed. "See you," he said, and hung up. He had another call to make.

He dialed J. D. Langley's number.

"Hello?" came the abrupt reply.

"I thought you were out of town," Calhoun said curtly.

"I was. I just got in fifteen minutes ago. I was having a cup of coffee. What's wrong?" he asked. "Something about the cattle?"

"Something about Fay York," Calhoun said.

There was a deathly hush. "Has anything happened to her?" he asked, feeling as if the ground had been cut out from under him. "Is she all right?"

Calhoun felt relieved. That was genuine concern in the other man's voice. Of course, and he hated himself for thinking of it, it could be that J.D. was counting on Fay's money to help him get his nephew. If he was, he was going to do Fay a big favor.

"I'm going to tell you something I'm not supposed to know," he said. "You aren't supposed to know it, either, so don't let on."

"What?"

"Fay didn't get a penny. Her father lost everything. All she inherits is the Mercedes."

J.D. didn't say anything, and Calhoun felt sorry for Fay. Until the sound of soft laughter came over the line and eased his mind.

"So she's busted," Donavan said warmly. "I had a feeling it would work out like that. I'm sorry for her, but I'm damned glad in a way. I wouldn't want people to think another Langley was taking the easy way out with a rich wife."

"You're really serious about her?" Calhoun asked, surprised.

"Why is that so hard to believe? You must have noticed that she's got a heart as big as all outdoors," he replied. Then he spoiled it all by adding, "She's just the kind of foster mother Jeff needs."

"You aren't going to marry her over a custody suit?"

"Whatever it is, is none of your business, Ballenger," J.D. said with icy politeness. "If Fay wants to marry me, that's her affair."

"And if she loves you, what then?"

"She isn't old enough to love anyone yet," Donavan said carelessly. "She's infatuated with me, and she needs a little security. I can give her enough to make her happy.''

Calhoun called him a name he wouldn't have wanted Abby to hear. ''You're lower than I gave you credit for,'' he added coldly.

''And it's still none of your damned business. I'll be in to check on the Mesa Blanco stock in the morning.'' He hung up, leaving Calhoun furious.

After hanging up on Calhoun, Donavan sipped his coffee without really tasting it. He was fond of Fay, and physically she appealed to him as no other woman had. She was innocent, and that alone excited him. He could make her happy.

But the thing was to get Jeff, to rescue the boy who was his sister's only child from the hell he was living in. It had taken all his powers of persuasion and a lot of tongue-biting to get his venomous brother-in-law to let Jeff come up here just for the spring holidays. Possession was nine-tenths of the law. He had Jeff and he was going to keep him. He'd already talked to the lawyer he shared with Mesa Blanco about filing for custody, so the wheels were turning.

''Are you sure you won't mind having me around, Uncle Don?'' Jeff asked from his sprawled position in the armchair. With his crewcut and husky physique, he looked the very picture of a boy who was all boy.

''No, sport, I won't,'' Donavan said. ''We get along pretty good most of the time.''

Jeff smiled. "Sure we do. Can we go riding tomorrow?"

"Maybe. First we have to go to the feedlot and check up on the feeder cattle. There's someone I want you to meet."

"Fay, right?" he asked, smiling again at his uncle's surprise. "She was all you talked about on the plane," he added.

Donavan lit a cigar and didn't look at the boy. He hadn't realized that he'd been so transparent. He'd missed Fay, but he didn't like admitting it even to himself. He'd been footloose all his life. Even if he married Fay for Jeff's sake, he didn't intend giving up his freedom.

"Aren't you going to call her?" Jeff asked.

"No," Donavan said, frowning. He did want to, but he wasn't going to give in to his impulse. Better to start the way he meant to go on, and acting like a boy with a crush wasn't going to keep him in control of his life.

"It's nice here," Jeff said after a minute. "I hate military school. You can't do anything without permission."

"Don't expect to be able to run wild here," his uncle cautioned.

"No, I don't. But you like me, at least. My stepfather hates my guts," he added coldly. "Especially now that he's married *her* and they're expecting their own child. He didn't even love my mother, did you know?"

Donavan's face hardened. "I knew," he said. He didn't elaborate on it, but he knew very well that his brother-in-law's blatant affairs had all but killed his sister. She'd loved the man, but his womanizing had depressed her to the point of madness. A simple case of pneumonia had taken her out of this world, out of her torment, leaving a heartbroken brother and son behind to mourn her. Donavan had hated Jeff's step-father ever since. Better his sister had stayed in mourning for her first husband than pitch headlong into a second marriage that was doomed from the start.

"What did she see in him?" Jeff asked miserably. "He drinks like a fish and he's always off somewhere. I think he's running around on his new wife already."

It wouldn't surprise Donavan. After all, he thought viciously, he was running around with his current wife while he was still married to Donavan's sister.

"Let's forget he exists for a few days," he told Jeff. "How about a game of chess?"

"Super!"

While Donavan and Jeff were playing chess, Fay was trying to come to grips with her new situation.

She'd always secretly wondered how she would cope if she ever lost everything. Now was her big chance, she thought with black humor, to find out. If she could conquer her fear of having her livelihood depend on her own efforts, she could manage. Thank goodness Donavan had made her take a good look at herself and start learning independence. If she'd still been living with Uncle Henry now, she really would have been terrified.

She understood now why her uncle had been so eager to push her at his business associate, Sean. It had been out of a misplaced protective instinct. He'd hoped she'd marry Sean and be secure when she found out there was nothing left of her parents' estate.

Even though she was grateful for his concern, she wished he'd told her sooner. She put her face in her hands. Well, she could always write to Great-Aunt Tessie and beg for help if things got too bad. She and the old lady had always kept in touch. In fact, there was no one else who loved Tessie just because of her sweet self and not her money. Fay always remembered the elderly woman's birthday. She wondered if anyone else ever had. Certainly not her parents.

She wiped the tears away and wondered when Donavan was coming back. He might not want her now. She had to face the fact that without her wealth, despite what he'd said about not wanting a wealthy woman, he might walk away without looking back. Time would tell. For now, she had enough to keep her busy. She got up from her chair and went to find the paperwork on the Mercedes. At least it would bring a tidy sum, and give her a badly needed nest egg.

The next morning after she'd dropped the papers off at Barry Holman's office, she was working away when the office door opened and Donavan Langley came in with a dark-haired boy at his side.

So he was back. And that had to be Jeff. Her heart ran wild, but she pinned a polite smile to her face as he approached her desk.

"Good morning," she said politely.

"This is Jeff," he replied without answering her. "Jeff, this is Fay York."

"Nice to meet you," Jeff said. He was watching her with open curiosity. "You're pretty."

She flushed. "Thank you."

Jeff grinned. "My uncle likes you."

"That's enough," Donavan drawled. "Go out and look at the cattle. But don't get in the way, and stay out of the pens."

"Yes, sir!"

He was off at a dead run, barely missing one of the amused cowboys. "Keep an eye on him, will you, Ted?" Donavan called.

"Sure thing, Mr. Langley," the cowboy replied, and turned on his heel to follow Jeff.

"He's impulsive and high tempered," Donavan told her. "I have to watch him like a hawk so that he doesn't hurt himself." He searched her eyes with no particular expression on his lean face, but his silver eyes were glittery with contained excitement. She stirred him up. He'd missed her more than he wanted to admit. But she wasn't receptive today. That smile was as artificial as the ficus plant in the pot beside her desk.

"Did you have a nice trip?" she asked for something to break the silence.

He nodded. "Jeff and I got in last night."

And he hadn't called. Well, now she knew where she stood. The fixed smile didn't waver, even if she had gone a shade paler. "He's a nice looking young man."

"He favors his mother. How about lunch? You can go with us to the hamburger joint."

She wanted to, but it was better to break this off now even if it killed her. Things could only get worse, and her life was in utter turmoil.

"I can't today, but thanks anyway."

He started. "Why can't you?"

"I have to see Mr. Holman about selling the Mercedes," she said with stiff pride. "You'll find out sooner or later, so I might as well tell you. I don't have any money. My parents left me without a dime." She lifted her chin and stared at him fearlessly. "All I have is the Mercedes and it's going on the market so that I'll have a nest egg for emergencies."

He didn't like the way she said that. She made it sound as if his only interest in her was what she had. Didn't she know it was her wealth that had stood between them in the first place?

He scowled. "The money didn't matter."

"Didn't it?" she asked bravely.

His gray eyes narrowed. "So you did believe Bart after all. You think I'm as money-crazy as my father." His expression went hard with contained rage. He'd thought she knew him better than that. It hurt to realize that she was just like several other people in Jacobsville who tarred him with the same brush they'd used on his father. "All right, honey. If that's the kind of man you think I am, then take your damned Mercedes and go to hell with it," he said cuttingly. He turned and went after Jeff.

Fay couldn't believe she'd said such a thing to him. Not that it would make any difference, she kept assuring herself. He didn't want her in the first place, so all she'd done was save herself a little more heartache.

Donavan didn't come back through the office on his way out. He took Jeff with him the back route, stormy and unapproachable, smoking his cigar like a furnace all the way to the car.

"What's eating you?" Jeff asked curiously.

"Nothing. What do you want for lunch?"

"A cheeseburger. I thought you said Fay was coming with us? Didn't she want to?"

"She was busy," he said curtly. "Get in."

Jeff shrugged. He wondered if he was ever going to understand adults.

Calhoun paused by Fay's desk, noticing her worn expression and trembling hands.

"J.D.'s been by, I gather," he said dryly.

She lifted her miserable eyes to his. "You might say that. He had Jeff with him."

"And left you here?"

She sat up straighter. "I told him I didn't have any money. He left."

He whistled. "Not a wise move, Fay," Calhoun said gently. "Donavan's touchy about money. You knew that his father—?"

"Yes, I knew," she cut him off gently. "It's for the best," she said. "He didn't really care about me. If he wanted me at all it was because he had a better chance of keeping Jeff if I was around. I'm not stupid. I know he doesn't love me."

Calhoun wanted to deny that, to reassure her, but it was patently obvious that she was right. J. D. Langley wasn't the hearts-and-roses type, but he sure didn't act like a man in love.

"It's early days yet," he told her, wanting to say something positive. "Give him time. J.D.'s been a loner ever since I've known him. He's a lot like Justin. Maybe that's why they get along so well. I have to admit, he and I have never been particularly friendly, but that doesn't have anything to do with you."

"I guess I should apologize," she began.

"Oh, not yet," he said, smiling. "Let him sweat for a while. It will do him good to be on the receiving end for once."

"You mean, he's usually the one who does the jilting," she said, sighing as she remembered how experienced he was. "I guess he's done his share of breaking hearts."

"Be careful of yours," Calhoun said seriously. "There's something I want to mention to you. I told you that this job was temporary, just until Nita came back." He hesitated, noticing her depressed look as she nodded. "Well, I want to offer it to you permanently. I need a secretary of my own, and Nita works a lot better with Justin than she does with me. What do you say? We've been thinking of adding a secretary, but until you came along, we weren't sure exactly what we wanted. You suit me and we seem to work pretty well together. Besides," he added on a chuckle, "Abby might divorce me if I let you go. She thinks a lot of you."

"I think a lot of her." Fay brightened magically. "You really mean it?"

"I mean it. If you want the job permanently, it's yours."

"And Nita won't mind working just for Justin?"

"I've already asked her. She almost kissed my feet. It seems that she's only been putting on a brave face about handling the workload for both of us. Getting some relief has given her a new lease on life. She said she was actually thinking of staying home with the baby just to get away from the work."

"Then I'd love the job, thank you," she said brightly. "You have no idea how much I enjoy working here. Besides," she confessed, not realizing that he already knew her situation, "I'm afraid I'm going to have to work for the rest of my life. My parents didn't leave me anything. I'm flat broke."

"In that case, we'll be helping each other out," he said. "So welcome aboard."

"Thanks, Calhoun," she said, and meant it. "Thanks very much."

"My pleasure."

She turned her attention back to her computer with an improved outlook. At least she had a job, even if she didn't have J. D. Langley. But that might still be for the best. She'd only have been letting herself in for a lot of heartache. It was better not to even begin something that was blighted from the start. And it wasn't as if he loved her. She had to keep remembering that.

The man driving back toward home was trying to keep it in mind himself, while he fumed inwardly at Fay's attitude. He wasn't mercenary, but she thought he was. Like father, like son. He groaned inwardly. Would he never be free of the stigma?

Jeff hadn't said a word, and Donavan couldn't bring himself to tell the boy why Fay wouldn't come to lunch with them. She thought he'd only been keeping company with her because of her money, when he'd already told her he didn't like rich women.

But in all honesty, he had to admit that he'd given her no real reason to think she was of value to him as a person. He'd talked much more about getting custody of Jeff than of wanting her for herself. He'd made love to her lightly, but even that could have convinced her that it was desire mingled with the need for a woman to aid his case to keep Jeff.

He frowned. He hadn't given her any chance at all. To compound it, he'd told her that he'd been back in town for almost a whole day and hadn't even bothered to phone her. He groaned inwardly. He'd made so many mistakes.

Worst of all, he hadn't considered her feelings. She'd just been told that she'd lost everything. All she had to her name was a Mercedes-Benz that she was going to have to sell. It was more than an inheritance she'd lost—it was her whole way of life. She had to be terrified at being responsible for herself. She was only twenty-one, and so alone, because she and her uncle weren't close. She'd needed comfort and help, and he'd told her to go to hell.

"You look terrible, Uncle Don," Jeff broke the tense silence. "Are you sure you're okay?"

"Not yet. But I will be," he said, and abruptly turned around in his own front yard and headed right back toward town. It was quitting time, so Fay would most likely be at home. He didn't know what he was going to say to her. He'd think of something.

Chapter Six

Fay had thought about staying late at the office, just to keep her mind busy, but in the end she decided she would be equally well-off at home. She said goodnight to her co-workers and drove the short distance back to her apartment house.

The Mercedes felt uncomfortable now that she was a working girl. It was just as well that Mr. Holman was going to help her sell it. There would be no more luxury cars, no more shopping sprees that didn't include looking at price tags. There would be no more designer clothes. No bottomless bank account to fall back on. She could have cried. She would make it. She knew she would. But getting used to her circumstances was going to take a little time.

She got out of the car and was walking onto the front porch when she heard the roar of a vehicle and saw Donavan driving up next to the Mercedes with Jeff beside him.

Not another fight, she prayed silently, her wan face resigned and miserable even if her eyes did light up helplessly at the very sight of him when he got out and approached her.

He stopped just in front of her, his own expression somber. She looked bad. The camouflage she'd hidden her fears behind had vanished now, because she was tired and her guard was down. He reached out and touched her mouth, dry and devoid of lipstick.

"I'm sorry," he said without preamble. "I didn't think about how you must feel until I was back home."

The unexpected compassion, on top of the emotional turmoil she'd been through, cracked inside her. Tears poured down her cheeks.

"I'm sorry, too," she managed brokenly. "Oh, Donavan, I didn't mean it...!"

His breath caught at her vulnerability, and he was glad he'd made the decision to come back. Without a word, he bent and lifted her in his hard arms and started back toward his car, kissing the tears away as he went, whispering comforting things that she didn't quite hear.

Jeff saw them coming and, with a grin, moved into the back seat. Donavan winked at him before he slid

Fay into the passenger seat and trussed her up in her seat belt.

"Stay put," he told her. "We're kidnapping you."

"What will my landlord think?" she asked with a watery smile.

"That you're being kidnapped, of course. We'll take her home and hold her prisoner until she cooks supper for us," he told Jeff, who was smiling from ear to ear. "If she's a good cook, I'll marry her right away."

Fay was trying not to choke. "But you told me to go to...!" she began.

"Not in front of the boy," he said with a mock glower. "He isn't supposed to know words like that."

"What century is *he* living in?" Jeff asked, rolling his eyes. "Gimme a break, man!"

"Too much TV," Donavan said. "We'll have to take a plug out of the set."

Fay's head was whirling. "But, Donavan, I can't cook. That is, I can," she faltered, wiping at her eyes. "But only omelets and bacon."

"No problem," he said as he started the car. "I like breakfast. Don't you, Jeff?"

"Sure!"

She gave up. In the scant minutes it took them to get to the ranch, she'd dried her tears and managed to gather her composure. She still didn't understand what had prompted Donavan to come after her, despite the way she'd insulted him, but she wasn't going to question a kindly fate.

Jeff was in a flaming rush to get to the living room for one of his favorite TV programs, leaving Donavan to escort a worn Fay into the kitchen.

"Mind Bee," he murmured, stepping around the kitten as she rushed toward them.

"I'll take care of her, Uncle Don," Jeff interrupted. He scooped up the kitten, popped back into the living room and closed the door behind him. The blare of the television could be heard even through it.

"The noise takes a little getting used to," Donavan said slowly. He studied Fay, whose hair was straggly as it came loose from its neat chignon. "Why do you wear it like that, anyway?" he asked gently, moving far too close to her. His lean hands deftly separated hairpins from upswept strands, loosening the dark cloud of her hair around her shoulders. "That's better," he whispered. "Now you look like my Fay again."

A tiny sob broke from her lips at the tenderness. Somehow she'd never associated it with him until now.

"I said such terrible things to you," she whispered back, her eyes eloquent.

"I said such terrible things back," he murmured, smiling. "We had a lovers' quarrel. Nothing to lose sleep over. Everything's all right now."

"We aren't lovers," she protested.

His eyes searched hers. "We're going to be, though."

She flushed. "I'm not like that."

He bent and drew his lips with aching tenderness over her own, gently parting them. His hands went to her hips and brought them firmly into the cradle of his, so that she could feel every vibrant muscle and tendon of him close, close against her softness.

"Come on, baby," he breathed into her open mouth. "Don't make me fight for it...."

She lost the will to protest the second she felt his tongue going past her lips, into the darkness beyond. A white-hot flash of sensation rippled her body in his arms, stiffened her. She caught her breath and then released it in a long, shuddering sigh that he could feel and taste.

"Yes," he said huskily. "That's it. That's it!"

He lifted her by the waist, turning her deftly to the wall. He pinned her there with his body, his long legs pushing between her thighs as he penetrated her mouth with quick, hard thrusts that simulated a kind of joining she'd never experienced.

When he finally lifted his head, she couldn't see anything except his swollen mouth. Her body was throbbing, like the tiny breaths that pulsed out of her, like her heart in her throat.

He leaned closer and bit her lower lip, not hard enough to hurt, but quite hard enough to make her aware of the violence of his passion.

She couldn't move. He had her pelvis completely under his, her legs supported by his, her breasts pinned beneath the heavy pressure of his chest. Behind her, the wall was cold and hard, not warm and alive like the man who had her helpless.

"I think you'd better marry me, Fay," he said huskily. "I don't know how much longer I can protect you."

"Protect me from what?" she asked, dazed by passion.

"Do you really need to ask?" he murmured against her bruised mouth.

"Marriage is a big step," she said weakly.

"Sure it is. But you and I are getting more explosive by the day. I want you like hell, honey, but not in the back seat of my car or some out-of-the-way motel when time permits. You're a virgin. That puts you right off limits."

"I'm poor," she said. "No, don't look like that," she pleaded, touching his thick eyebrows where they clashed to smooth away the scowl. "I mean, I'd be a burden on you. I'll work, but I can't make much..."

"How do you think other couples manage?" he asked. "For God's sake, I don't care if you're poor! So am I, in a lot of ways. You're much more desirable to me without money than you were with it, and I think you know why."

"Yes. I shouldn't have said what I did. I was so afraid that you wouldn't want me anymore."

He lifted an eyebrow. "Does it feel like I don't want you?" he asked pleasantly.

He hadn't moved, but what he felt was rather blatant and she blushed.

He laughed softly as he let her slide down against him until her feet touched the floor. He loomed over her as he searched her flushed face with indulgent amusement.

"You're priceless," he murmured. "Will you faint on our wedding night, or hide in the bathroom? I'll wager you've never seen a naked man, much less an aroused one."

"I guess I'll get used to it," she replied gamely.

He chuckled. "I guess you'll have to. Yes or no?"

She took a deep breath. "Yes, then," she said, refusing to worry about his motives or even her own. She wanted him and he wanted her. She'd worry about the rest of the problems later.

He didn't speak for so long that she was frankly worried that he was regretting the proposal. Then he lifted her hands to his mouth and kissed them with breathless tenderness, and the look in his silver eyes made her feel humble. Whatever he felt right now, it wasn't reluctance. Her heart lifted and flew.

Jeff was called in minutes later and told the news. He literally jumped for joy.

"When?" he asked them.

Fay hesitated. Donavan didn't. "Next week," he said, his eyes daring Fay to challenge him.

"Then," Jeff said, as if he was reluctant to put it into words, "can I stay for the wedding?"

Donavan studied him in a silence that became more tense by the second. "As far as I'm concerned, you can stay until you're of legal age."

"That goes for me, too," Fay said without prompting.

Jeff looked embarrassed. He colored and averted his eyes. Like his uncle, very little showed in his face unless he wanted it to. But his uneasiness was a dead giveaway.

"I'd like that," Jeff said. "But wouldn't I be in the way?"

"No," Donavan said tersely. "We won't have time for a honeymoon right away, and you'll need to be registered in school here, even though it's almost the end of the school year."

Jeff's eyes widened. "You mean I won't have to go back to military school?"

"Not unless you want to," Donavan told him. "I've already started custody proceedings for you."

"Gosh, Uncle Don," Jeff said enthusiastically. "I don't even know what to say!"

"Say okay and go back and watch television with Bee," Donavan mused, glancing warmly at Fay. "I haven't finished kissing Fay yet."

"Oh. That mushy stuff," Jeff said with a sly grin.

"That mushy stuff," Donavan agreed, smiling at Fay's wild-rose blush. "You'll understand in a few years."

"Don't bet on it," the boy murmured. He reached down to retrieve Bee, who was tangling his shoelaces. "I'd like to stay here," he said without looking at them. "I'd like it a lot. But my stepdad won't ever agree."

"Let me worry about that," Donavan told him. "We'll call you when supper's ready."

"Okay. I won't hold my breath or anything, though," he added dryly, and closed the door behind him.

Fay stared up at Donavan and felt as if every dream she'd ever had was about to come true. She had nothing. But if she had Donavan, she had the world.

She said so. He looked briefly uncomfortable. She didn't know that he was unsure of his own reasons for wanting to marry her. He wanted to keep Jeff. He felt a furious physical longing to make love to Fay. But beyond that, he was afraid to speculate. He'd done without love all his life. He wasn't sure he knew what it was.

"I haven't embarrassed you?" she asked worriedly.

He moved forward and drew her slowly into his arms. "No," he said. His eyes searched hers. "It's going to be hard for you getting used to my life-style. I like my own way. I budget like a madman. There's no provision for pretty dresses and expensive cosmetics and a trip to the hairdresser once a week . . ."

Daringly, she put her fingers against his hard mouth. "I won't miss those things." She traced his lean cheek and his firm mouth and chin, loving the way he tolerated her exploration. "Oh, glory," she said on an unsteady breath. "I'll get to sleep with you every night."

He stiffened at the way she said it, as if being in his arms would lift her right up to heaven. He brought her closer and bent to kiss her with slow, expert thoroughness.

She reached up to hold him back, giving in with exquisite delight pulsing through her body, loving him as she'd never dreamed she could love someone.

He lifted his head feverish seconds later and clasped her shoulders firmly while he looked down at her. "I hope I'm going to be man enough to satisfy you in bed," he said on a husky laugh. "You are one wild little creature, Fay."

She flushed. "I hope that's a compliment."

"It's a compliment, all right," he replied, fighting for enough breath to talk. She confounded him. For an innocent, which he was almost certain she was, there was no reticence in her when he started kissing her. She made his knees weak. In bed, she was going to be the end of his rainbow.

She studied him with soft, worried green eyes. "I haven't ever slept with anyone," she began nervously.

He smiled gently. "I know that. But you've got promise, honey. A lot of it." He leaned close and brushed his lips over her nose. "I'm glad it's going to be with me, Fay," he whispered huskily. "Your first time, I mean."

Her heart ran wild. "So am I."

His lips probed gently at her mouth, teasing it open. "Do you know what to expect?" he breathed.

"I . . . think so."

His eyes opened at point-blank range, silver fires that burned while she felt his coffee-scented breath on her lips. "I've never been gentle," he whispered. "But I will be. With you."

"Donavan," she breathed, her eyes closing as she pulled him down to her.

He didn't know if he was going to survive the soft heat of her body, the clinging temptation of her mouth. He groaned under his breath as the kiss went on and on, burning into his very soul.

"I can't bear it," he groaned at her lips. "Fay . . . !"

The tormented sound gave her the willpower to pull gently out of his arms and move away. Her knees felt weak, but he looked as if he was having a hard time standing up straight.

"It's like being thirsty, isn't it?" she asked breathlessly. "You can't quite get enough to drink."

"Yes." He turned away from her and lit a cigar with hands that were just faintly unsteady.

She stared at his long back lovingly, at the body that would one day worship hers. He was going to be her man, her very own. Losing her fortune seemed such a tiny sacrifice to make to have Donavan for the rest of her life.

She smiled to herself. "If you'll show me where the eggs are, I'll make you and Jeff an omelet," she offered. "I'm sorry I can't cook anything else just yet, but I'll learn."

"I know that. Don't worry about it," he added with a fairly calm smile. "I can cook."

"You can teach me," she mused.

"To cook," he agreed. His eyes fell to the visible tautness of her breasts. "And other things."

She smiled with barely contained excitement as she followed him to the refrigerator.

Supper was a gleeful affair, with Jeff laughing and joking with his uncle and Fay as if he'd never had a solemn, sad day in his life. He rode back with them when Donavan eventually drove Fay home and sat in the car while they walked to the door of Fay's apartment house.

"I can't believe the change in Jeff," he remarked as they paused on the darkened porch. "He's not the same boy who came out here with dead eyes and even deader dreams."

"Does his stepfather care about him?"

"Not so anyone would notice," he replied. "He was always jealous of the way my sister got along with Jeff, always resentful of him. He made Jeff's life hell from the very beginning. Since my sister died, it's been much worse."

"Will he fight you over custody, do you think?"

"Oh, I'm convinced of it," Donavan said lightly. "That's all right. I don't mind a good fight."

"That's what I've heard," she murmured dryly.

He chuckled. "I grew up swinging. Had to. My father made sure of that." His eyes darkened and the smile faded. "You'll have that to live down, too, if you marry me. Some people won't know that you've lost your inheritance. There will be talk."

"I don't mind," she murmured. "While they're talking about me, they'll be leaving someone else alone."

"You don't get depressed much, do you?" he asked quizzically.

"I used to, before you came along." She toyed with a button of his shirt, loving the feel of him close to her, the warm strength of his hands on her shoulders. She looked up, her eyes shadowed in the darkness of the porch. "I'm much too happy now to be depressed."

He frowned. "Fay...I've been alone a long time. Jeff's taking some getting used to. A wife...well, I may make things difficult for you at first."

"Just as long as you don't have women running through the house in towels or anything," she said with an impish smile.

He chuckled. "No chance of that. I've kept to myself in recent years." He bent and brushed her mouth lightly with his, refusing to let the kiss ignite this time. "Good night, little one. Jeff and I will pick you up for lunch tomorrow."

"Cheeseburgers, right?"

"Right," he murmured. "I wish we were already married, Fay, and that we were completely alone. I'd carry you up those steps and take an hour stripping the clothes off you."

"Hush!" she giggled. "I don't wear *that* many!"

"You don't understand, do you?" he whispered. "You will."

"That first time we went out, you wouldn't even kiss me," she recalled suddenly.

"I didn't dare. I wanted it too much." He smoothed back her hair. "I figured you'd be addictive, Fay. I was right, wasn't I?"

"I'm glad I am," she said fervently.

"So am I. Good night, sweet."

He turned and left her, and he didn't look back, not even when he'd started the car and drove away. Jeff waved, and she waved back. But Donavan hadn't even glanced in the rearview mirror.

It made her nervous, realizing that he didn't seem to look back. Was it an omen? Was she doing the right thing to marry a man whose only feeling for her was desire?

She worried it all night, but by morning, the only thing she was certain of was that she couldn't live without Donavan. She went into the office resolute, determined to make the best of the situation.

"Is it true?" Abby asked the minute she came in the door later that morning, looking and sounding breathless.

Fay didn't have to ask any questions. She laughed. "If you mean, am I going to marry J. D. Langley, yes."

"Fay, you're crazy," Abby said gently. She sat down beside the younger woman. "Listen, he wants custody of Jeff, that's all. I'll absolve him of wanting your money, but if you think he's marrying you for love..."

Fay shook her head. "No, I'm not that crazy," she assured her friend. "But I care too much to refuse," she added quietly. "He may learn to love me one day. I have to hope that he will."

"It's not fair," Abby argued worriedly.

"It's fair to Jeff," Fay reminded her. "He stands to lose so much if he has to go back to live with his stepfather. He's a great boy, Abby. A boy with promise."

"Yes, I know. I've met him." She sat down on the edge of Fay's desk with a long sigh. "I hope you know what you're doing. I can't see J.D. passionately in love. Calhoun said he was actually cussing you when he left here yesterday."

"He was," she replied dryly. "And I was giving as good as I got. But we made up later."

Abby raised an eyebrow at the blush. "So I see."

"I can't say no, regardless of his reasons for wanting to marry me," Fay said urgently. "Abby, I love him."

The older woman didn't have an argument left. She looked at Fay and saw herself several years before, desperately in love with Calhoun and living on dreams. She knew that she'd have done anything Calhoun had asked, right down to living with him.

She smiled indulgently. "I know how that feels," she said finally. "But I hope you're doing the right thing."

"Oh, so do I!" Fay said with heartfelt emotion.

When Donavan came to pick her up for lunch, the office was empty. Calhoun and Abby had their midday meal together most of the time, and the office girls took an early lunch so that they could be back during the regular lunch hour.

"Where's Jeff?" she asked, surprised that the boy wasn't with him.

"Gone to the movies," Donavan told her, smiling. "He thinks engaged people need some time alone. That being the case," he murmured, tugging her up by one hand, "suppose we buy the ingredients for a pic-

nic lunch and find a secluded spot down by the river
where we can make love to each other after we eat?''

She blushed, smiling at him with her whole heart.
''Okay.''

He chuckled as he pulled her along with him,
standing aside to let the first of the office crew back in
the building before he escorted her out to his car.

''We're raising eyebrows,'' he murmured. ''Do they
know we're engaged?''

''Everybody seems to,'' she replied.

''Small town gossip. Well, it doesn't matter, does
it?''

She shook her head. ''Not at all.''

They stopped by a grocery store in a nearby shopping center and bought lunch at the take-out deli,
adding soft drinks and ice for a small cooler. It wasn't
a fancy or expensive lunch, but Fay felt as if it were
sheer elegance.

''You look like one of those posed pictures of a
debutante at a garden party,'' he remarked, his eyes on
the way her gauzy white-and-green patterned dress
outlined her body as she lay across from him on a spot
of grass.

''I feel that way, too,'' she mused, tossing her long
hair as she arched her back and sighed. Her eyes
closed. ''It's so peaceful here.''

''If that's a complaint...''

The sound of movement brought her eyes open just
in time to find Donavan levering his jean-clad body

over hers. He was smiling, but there was a kind of heat in the smile that made her body begin to throb.

His elbows caught his weight as he eased down on top of her, his long legs cradling hers in a silence tense with promise. His eyes dropped to her mouth.

"This is as good a time as any for you to start getting used to me," he whispered. His hips shifted slowly, first to one side, then to the other. The faint movement aroused him and he tensed as the familiar heat shot through him like fire.

Fay watched his face contort slightly even as she felt the changing contours of his body. Her lips parted on a held breath.

"A hundred years or so ago, when I was young and hot-blooded, that was a frequent and worrying occurrence. These days," he mused, watching her flushed face, "it's more of a delightful surprise. I like the way my body reacts to you."

"It doesn't . . . react to other women like this?" she asked, torn between embarrassment and curiosity.

He shook his head. "Only to you, apparently. I must be getting old. Either that, or a diet of virginal shock is rejuvenating me."

"It isn't shock. Well, not exactly," she faltered.

"No?" He bent and gently parted her lips. One long, powerful leg began to ease its way between hers, parting them and spreading her skirt on the cool ground. He felt her gasp and lifted his head. "We don't have a lot of time for courtship," he breathed.

"We need to get used to each other physically before we marry. It will make it easier."

"I've never done this," she said nervously.

"Not even this far?" he asked, surprised.

She shook her head. "My parents were very strict. So were the relatives I used to stay with. They all said it was a sin to let a man do what he liked to a woman's body."

"Perhaps in some respects it is," he replied quietly. "But you and I are going to be married. One day, I'm going to put my seed deep in your body and you're going to have my baby. That won't be a sin of any kind."

The words, so carelessly spoken, had a very uncareless reaction on Fay. Her eyes went wide and watchful, and her face went scarlet.

He felt her sudden tension, saw it in her face. "That excites you, does it?" he whispered huskily. His eyes fell to her breasts, and he watched the nipples go hard with quiet pride before he caught her shocked eyes again. "You have pretty breasts."

The blush exploded and he chuckled. "I shouldn't tease you, Fay. Not about something so profound. But it's irresistible. As irresistible as . . . this."

And as he spoke, he bent suddenly and put his open mouth over the hard tip of her breast.

Chapter Seven

Fay thought that if she died and flew into the sun she couldn't have felt any greater explosion of heat. The feel of Donavan's hot mouth on her body, even through the cloth, was incredible.

She arched against him and made a sound, half gasp, half groan, while her nails bit into his hard shoulders.

His teeth nipped her delicately, before his tongue began to swirl around the hard tip and make it unbearably sensitive to the moist heat of his mouth.

"Please," she whispered huskily. "Please, please, please ... !"

He barely heard her through his own need. His fingers were quick and rough on her bodice, painful sec-

onds passing before he managed to disarrange the
hated fabric that kept her soft skin from his mouth.
He found her with his lips and his hands simulta-
neously, and she clung to him, no thought of protest
in her whirling mind as she fed on the feverish tasting
of his mouth, the hot sensuality of his hands on her
body.

"Don . . . avan!" she sobbed.

He lifted his head abruptly and looked at her.

"My God, you're beautiful, Fay," he said unsteadily. "The most beautiful creature unclothed that I've
ever seen in my life!"

"I want you," she said weakly.

"I want you, too."

"Here."

He shook his head, fighting for sanity. He had to
drag his eyes away from her body to meet her own.
"No. Not now. We aren't married, little one."

"It . . . doesn't matter!" she wept, her body racked
with need.

"Yes, it does." Gently he disengaged her hands and
put her clothing to rights. When she was dressed
again, he rolled onto his back and pulled her down
into his arms. He held her while she cried, his voice
soothing, his hands gentling her while the storm
passed.

"I'm a lucky man, Fay," he said when she was quiet
again. "A very lucky man."

"I think I'm the lucky one," she said breathlessly, clinging.

He bent and kissed her, his silver eyes looking straight into hers while his lean hands framed her flushed face gently. "We're taking a big step together," he said then, and looked solemn. "I hope for both our sakes, and Jeff's, that it's the right one."

"It will be," she assured him. Somehow, she knew it. But it didn't escape her notice that he looked unconvinced.

The next week went by in a pleasant haze. Fay spent every free moment with Donavan and Jeff, taking just time enough to go shopping with Abby for her wedding gown. She chose an oyster-hued suit, which was sensible, because it would go with everything she had left in her wardrobe. She splurged on a hat, too, and a veil to drape over it. She worried about the amount of money she'd spent, because it was no longer possible to buy without looking at price tags. But Donavan only smiled when she mentioned that, and told her that getting married certainly warranted a little splurging.

The ceremony was held at the local church where Donavan was a member, and half the population of Jacobsville turned out for the occasion. Most everyone knew by now that Fay had lost everything, and even Donavan's cousin Bart was civil to him.

Jeff stayed with the Ballengers while Donavan drove himself and his new bride all the way to San Antonio for their two-day honeymoon. They had supper on the paseo del rio, where lighted barges went past with mariachi bands and music filled the flower-scented air.

"There can't be any place on earth more beautiful than this," she commented when she finished the last bite of her apple pie à la mode and looked at her new husband with quiet possession.

He cocked an eyebrow, very handsome in the pale gray suit he'd worn to be married in. He hadn't changed. Neither had she. She was still wearing her off-white suit, because they hadn't wanted to take the time to change earlier.

"Aren't you disappointed that I couldn't offer you a week in Nice or St. Tropez?"

She smiled and shook her head. "I'm very happy. I hope I can make you that way, too."

His returning smile became slowly wicked. "Suppose I take you back to our room now? I want to see how many times I can make you blush before I show you what physical love is."

Her heart beat faster. "All right," she whispered with barely contained excitement, and was unable to meet his eyes as he paid the bill and led her out into the sweetly scented night.

"Are you afraid of it, Fay?" he asked in the elevator, where they were briefly alone.

"A little, I think," she confessed with a nervous laugh. She looked up at him. "I don't want to disappoint you. I know you aren't innocent..."

He smiled gently. "I've never been married, though," he reminded her. "Or had a virgin to initiate." The smile faded. "I'll try not to hurt you too much."

"Oh, I'm not worried about...that," she faltered.

"Aren't you?" he mused knowingly as the elevator stopped.

They entered the room and he locked the door behind them, but when her cold hand went toward the light switch, he caught it.

"It will be easier for you in the dark," he whispered as he brought her gently close. "I don't want you to see me just yet."

"Do you have warts?" She laughed, trying to make a joke of it.

"No. You'll understand a lot better in the morning. For now," he said, swinging her up in his arms as he started toward the bed, "let's enjoy each other."

She'd never dreamed that she could lie quietly while a man took her clothes off, but she did. Donavan made what could have been an ordeal into a breathless anticipation, kissing her between buttons and catches, stroking her body gently to relax her while he slowly and deftly removed every stitch she had on. Then he pulled her against him, and she felt the faint abrasion of his suit while he began to kiss her.

"You . . . you're still dressed," she whispered.

He bit at her mouth with lazy delight. "I noticed. Open your mouth a little more. That's it." He kissed her very slowly and his hand smoothed down over her taut breasts, making her gasp, before it left a warm trail down her flat belly to the soft inside of her thighs. "Don't faint," he whispered as he touched her intimately for the first time and felt her tense. "Relax, Fay," he breathed at her lips as he trespassed beyond even her wildest and most erotic dreams. She cried out and he made a rough sound, deep in his throat. "My God, this isn't going to be the best night of your life. Listen, sweetheart, do you want to wait until you can see a doctor?" he asked, lifting his head. "I don't want to frighten you, but this barrier isn't going to be easily dispensed with. You know, don't you, that I'm going to have to break it before I can take you?"

"Yes." She swallowed. "Will it hurt you, too, if you do?"

"More than likely." He rolled onto his back and pulled her close, his body pulsating with its denied need while he fought his inclination to say to hell with it and go ahead. He needed her, but he didn't want to hurt her, to make intimacy something that would frighten and scar her.

"I didn't know," she said hesitantly. "I've never had any female problems, and I didn't think I needed a prenuptial checkup . . ."

He smoothed her long hair gently. "I'm not fussing, am I?" he murmured.

"I'll bet you feel like it," she said miserably. She laughed and then began to cry. "I've ruined everything!"

"Don't be absurd." His arms tightened and he rolled over against her, his mouth warm and soft and slow as his hand moved down her body again. Instead of probing, this time it touched, lightly, sensually. She gasped and instinctively caught his hand, but it was already too late. The pleasure caught her by surprise and for minutes that seemed never to end, she was oblivious to everything except her husband.

A long time later, he got up, leaving her wide-eyed and more than a little shaken on the bed. He turned the lights on and looked at his handiwork, from the drowsy, sated green eyes to the pink luxury of her sprawled body. She was too fulfilled to even protest the intimacy now, and his expression was just faintly smug.

"No need to ask if you liked it," he murmured unforgivably and began to take off his clothes.

She watched him with visible pleasure. He had a stunning body, very powerful and darkly tanned, except for a pale band where she imagined his swimming trunks normally rested. He was lightly feathered all over with dark, curling hair, except for his chest and flat stomach, where it was thickest. He turned toward her and she caught her breath, unable to take her eyes off him. Even like this, he was any woman's dream. Especially like this.

He knelt over her, his eyes glittering with unsatisfied desire. "Now it's my turn," he whispered, easing down beside her. "I want what I gave you."

"Anything," she choked. "Teach me . . . !"

His mouth covered hers, and lessons followed that banished her shyness, her fear, her inhibitions. When he cried out a second time and was still, she lay against him with drowsy pleasure and closed her eyes in satisfied sleep.

They went back home the next morning. Donavan murmured dryly that he wasn't spending another night playing at sex when they could have the real thing after she saw the doctor. She did, first thing Monday morning, although the minor surgery was a little embarrassing. The doctor was pleased at Donavan's care, because, he added, it would have been an unpleasant experience for both of them if her new husband had been impatient. He sent her home with a smile and she dreamed for the three days it took for the discomfort to pass.

It was going to be the most exciting night of Donavan's life, Fay promised herself as she got everything ready. She'd already asked Abby to keep Jeff for that one evening, without telling her why, and Jeff had agreed with a murmured dry remark about newlyweds needing some privacy. Nobody knew that the marriage hadn't been consummated. But tonight it was going to be.

Fay had a bottle of champagne chilling. She'd cooked a special meal and made a crepe dessert, things she'd had Abby show her how to do. Everything looked delicious. Even Fay, who was wearing one of the only sexy dresses she possessed, a little strappy black satin number that showed off her full breasts and her long, elegant legs in the nicest possible way. She'd left her hair loose around her shoulders, the way Donavan liked it, and sprayed herself with perfume. He'd been exquisitely patient and caring for the past few nights, contenting himself with a few gentle kisses and the feel of her in his arms and nothing more. Tonight, she was going to make him glad he'd been so considerate.

She heard his car pull up in the driveway, very impatiently, and heard the vicious slam of his door. Something must have upset him at work, she thought as she quickly lit the candles on the table. Well, she had the cure for that.

She turned as he threw open the front door and came in. That was when she realized that what had upset him wasn't the job. He was staring at her with undisguised fury, his whole look accusing and violent.

"You didn't tell me you had a great-aunt who could buy and sell Miami Beach."

She blinked and had to think hard. "You mean Great-Aunt Tessie," she faltered. "Well, yes, but..."

His face hardened. His lean hand almost crushed the hat he'd just swept from his damp hair. "Your uncle Henry had a call a few minutes ago. He wanted me to break the news to you." He took a steadying breath. "Your great-aunt died last night. You inherit everything she owned, and that includes millions of dollars."

He was white in the face. Now she knew why. She sat down heavily. "Tessie is dead? But I had a letter from her just last week. She was fine..."

"You didn't tell me," he ground out. "Why?"

She lifted her eyes. "I never thought of it. Honestly," she said dully. Tears stung her eyelids. She'd been very fond of Tessie. "I loved her. Her money never made any difference to me. I expected she'd leave it to charity. She knew I didn't need it."

"Didn't, as in past tense." He nodded. "But now you're not a woman of property. Or are you?"

"I can always refuse it," she began.

"Don't bother. I assume you'll want to fly down there," he said shortly. "Your uncle will go with you. He said he'd make the travel arrangements and let you know later." He tugged at his tie, glaring at her.

"It's not my fault," she said huskily, tears pouring down her cheeks.

"Don't you think I know that?" he replied, his eyes cold and dark. "But it changes everything. I won't stay married to you. Not now."

"What about Jeff?" she gasped. "The custody suit?"

"I don't know..."

He was uncharacteristically hesitant. She went closer to him. "We don't have to tell anyone," she said. "I'll swear Uncle Henry to secrecy. We can stay married long enough for you to get Jeff away from his stepfather. Then we can get a . . . a divorce."

"Divorce?" he asked with a curt laugh. "An annulment." She flushed. "Had you forgotten, baby?" he asked mockingly. "We played at sex, but we never had it. Now it's just as well that we didn't. No harm done. You can find yourself some society boy in your own circle and get married again."

"And you?"

He shrugged indifferently and turned away before she could see his face. "I'll have Jeff."

"You don't want me?"

"What I want or don't want doesn't enter into it anymore," he said coolly, careful not to let her see his face. "The last thing I can afford is to have Jacobsville start gossiping about another Langley marrying for money, especially when I've got Jeff's future to think about."

"Oh, I see."

She did, painfully. Donavan would never want her
with millions. He was a proud man. Much too proud
to withstand the snide remarks and gossip. Even if he
was less proud, there was Jeff. The boy shouldn't have
to suffer for things he'd never done.

"I'll . . . just phone Uncle Henry," she said, but
Donavan didn't answer her. He went out and closed
the door.

The next morning, he drove her and her uncle to the
airport and put them on a plane. The Ballengers had
been very understanding about her absence from work
for a couple of days, and Abby was glad to fill in for
her under the circumstances. They all put down Fay's
apathy to her fondness for her great-aunt, so it was
just as well they didn't see her with Donavan. His
fierce scowl might have changed their minds.

"Thanks for driving us here," Henry said uncom-
fortably. "Fay, I'll wait for you on the concourse."

"Yes." She watched him go with dull eyes before
she lifted her own to Donavan.

"You haven't slept, have you?" he asked formally.
And he had to ask, because he'd moved out of her
bedroom the night before without a word.

She shook her head. "I was fond of Great-Aunt
Tessie. We were good friends."

"I wasn't very sympathetic last night," he said
stiffly. "I'm sorry . . ."

Her chin lifted proudly. "I haven't asked for anything from you, have I, Donavan?" she asked with expression. "And I won't. I'll stay with you until the custody hearing. Then, as you suggested, we can get an annulment."

"What will you do?" he asked.

She only laughed. She felt a million years old. "What do you care?" she asked without looking at him. She picked up the case he'd been carrying for her. "I haven't told the Ballengers about what I'll inherit, and I hope you won't," she said over her shoulder. "Until I talk to her lawyers, nothing is really certain."

"Don't make some stupid decision about that money out of misplaced loyalty to me," he said coldly, forcing himself to smile as if he didn't give a damn about her. Letting her give up millions to live a modest life-style with him, out of nothing but desire, would be criminal. "I only married you to get Jeff. Maybe I wanted you, too," he added when she looked at him. "But bodies come cheap, honey. I've never gone hungry."

Her face went, if possible, a shade paler. "It's nice to know that I'll be leaving you heart-whole and unencumbered. Goodbye, Donavan."

"Not goodbye," he said carelessly. "So long."

She shook her head. "No, I meant it. I'll come back. I'll stay, for Jeff. But in every other way, it's goodbye." Her eyes fell away from his and she tried not to feel the bitter wound of rejection that made her insides hurt. Every step was one less she'd have to repeat. She thought about that as she counted them. She didn't look back, either. She was learning, as he apparently already had, not to ever look back.

The trip to Miami was long and tiresome. She and Uncle Henry spent two days dealing with Great-Aunt Tessie's possessions, saving keepsakes and arranging for disposal of everything else. The very last stop was the lawyer's office, where Fay sat beside her uncle with dead eyes, hardly aware of her surroundings.

"I know the will seems cut-and-dried," the attorney said apologetically, glancing at Fay and grimacing, "but I'm afraid it was altered just recently without my knowledge. Tessie's maid found the new will in her bedside table, witnessed and properly signed."

Henry's eyebrows raised. "Did she leave the whole shooting match to her cats?" he asked with a chuckle.

"Oh, it's a little better than that," the attorney returned, reading over the document. "She left it to open a chain of hostels that would house the families of children with incurable cancer. It seems her housekeeper's sister had a child with leukemia and was having to drive a hundred miles a day back and forth because she couldn't afford to stay in a hotel... Mrs. Langley, are you all right?"

Fay was aghast. Delighted. Unbearably pleased. She looked at the attorney. "You mean, I don't have to take the money?"

Her wording shocked him, when very little ever had. "You don't want it!"

"Oh, no," she agreed. "I'm quite happy as I am."

"Well, I'm not," Henry muttered. "She could have left me a few sticks of furniture or something."

"But she did," the attorney recovered himself enough to add. "There's a provision for the contents of her apartment to be sold at public auction and the proceeds split between the two of you. I should say it will amount to very nearly a quarter of a million dollars. There is, too, her jewelry, which she wanted to go to Mrs. Langley—provided none of it is sold. Heirlooms, you know."

Fay smiled. "Some of the pieces date back three hundred years to European royal houses. I'd never sell it. It should go to descendants." She realized that she wouldn't have any now, and her face fell.

"At least we got something," Henry told her once they were outside. "I don't feel so bad that your inheritance didn't come through, now."

"There was nothing you could have done," Fay assured him. "I don't have any hard feelings."

He stared at her curiously. "You didn't want Tessie's money?"

She shook her head as they walked back to the rented car. "Not at all. Donavan would never have married me in the first place if I'd been rich."

"Yes. He does have a sore spot about his father." He glanced at her. "Well, this slight in Tessie's will should make your marriage a little more stable. I can imagine what J. D. Langley would have thought if you'd inherited all that money."

"Yes. Can't you, though?" Although she was thinking that if he'd loved her, money wouldn't have mattered at all. He'd tossed her out on her ear because he thought she was inheriting Tessie's money. He didn't want her rich. Well, that was all right with her. A relationship based on money—no matter if it was too much or too little—wasn't the right kind. She'd go on with her job at the feedlot and tell him that her inheritance was going to be tied up for a time. Beyond that, he didn't really need to know anything else. He'd thrown her out. She had to consider that maybe he'd done her a favor. She was falling more in love with him by the day. But aside from his need to keep Jeff and his desire for her, there was nothing on his side worth fighting for. As he'd already said, he could have all the women he needed. What would he want with Fay?

She did feel somewhat responsible for Jeff, though, since she'd agreed to the marriage in the first place partly to help rescue him from his stepfather. She liked the boy. For his sake, she wasn't going to walk out on

J. D. Langley. She'd stick with them until the court case was settled one way or the other. Then she'd make whatever decisions had to be made.

It was ironic, though, that she'd gone to her marriage bed a virgin and left it still a virgin, even if she had learned quite a lot about pleasure in the process. She wondered if she could get into *The Guinness Book of Records?*

She packed her things and got ready to head back to Jacobsville. She didn't seem fated to be rich anymore, and she was rather glad about it. It was one thing to be born into money, quite another to learn to make it in the world without a big bankroll to fall back on.

If Donavan had loved her, she'd have had everything. She remembered so many good times with him, so much sweetness and pleasure. He'd genuinely seemed to like her at times, and his desire for her had been quite unmistakable. But desire wasn't love.

She couldn't settle for a man who looked at her as an infrequent dessert that he could live without. She wanted to be loved as well as wanted, to be cherished just for herself. Donavan had put conditions on their relationship that she couldn't meet. Be poor and I'll want you, he'd as good as said. If he'd loved her, whether she was rich or poor wouldn't have mattered. And all the gossip in the world wouldn't have made any difference.

Donavan had never loved, so he couldn't know that. But Fay did. She had to go back to him now and pretend that she didn't love him, that they were simply two people living together for the sake of a child. They weren't even legally married, because the marriage hadn't been consummated. She laughed bitterly. Jeff's stepfather could have had plenty of fun with that charge in court, but nobody knew except Donavan and herself, thank God.

She closed the case she'd been packing and went to phone the bellhop station. She had to go home and face Donavan, and the future.

Chapter Eight

When Fay and her uncle arrived at the airport, it was a shock to find Donavan waiting for them.

She shot a curious glance at her uncle, but he looked as surprised as she did.

"We could have gotten a cab," she began, her very calm voice belying the turmoil that the sight of Donavan engendered in her.

"It was no hardship to pick you up," he said easily. He was smoking a cigar, wearing working clothes that were clean if not new. His Stetson was cocked over one eye so that it wasn't possible to see the expression on his lean face. Just as well, too, he thought, because he wasn't ready for Fay to find out how glad he was to see her. The days had been endless since she

left, and his conscience was hurting him. He'd been
unkind to her at a time when she'd needed compassion and a shoulder to cry on.

"This is decent of you, Donavan," Henry said as he
shouldered cases and followed Donavan out to the car.
"I hate cabs."

Fay didn't comment. She clutched her purse and her
overnight bag tightly, not returning Donavan's quiet,
close scrutiny. She didn't care what he did or said
anymore, she told herself. He'd hurt her for the very
last time.

He dropped Henry off and not a word was spoken
until he escorted Fay into the house.

"Jeff's in school," he told her when she noticed the
sudden hush in the house. Only Bee, the kitten, was in
evidence when Donavan came back from depositing
her bags in her room. He picked her up with a faint
smile and deposited her in a chair.

"You enrolled Jeff in school here, then?" she
asked.

"Yes." He stopped just in front of her, his silver
eyes probing as he looked down at her in the off-white
suit she'd been married in. It brought back painful
memories.

"How are you?" he asked.

"Still kicking," she replied dryly. "I'm not bleed-
ing, Donavan, so you don't need to worry over me. I
won't be a problem. Now, if you'll excuse me, I'll un-

pack and change. Then I'll see about starting something for supper."

"You don't have to. . ." he began irritably.

"I don't mind." She turned away, cutting him off before he could sway her resolve. "You've said it all already," she added without turning. "Let's just leave it alone. Have you heard from your lawyer about the custody hearing?"

"Yes," he said after a minute. "It's scheduled for next week."

She didn't know what else to say, so she nodded and left him there. It was some small consolation that he seemed as ill at ease as she felt. Their marriage was over before it had even had a chance to begin. She wished they could start again. But she doubted that Donavan believed in second chances any more than she did herself.

It was a silent meal. Jeff looked from one of them to the other with curiosity and faint uneasiness.

"I'm sorry about your great-aunt, Fay," Jeff said when they were eating the pudding she'd made for dessert. "I guess you're still sad."

"Yes," she agreed without argument. "Great-Aunt Tessie was special. She was a renegade in a day and age when it wasn't popular."

"Was she really rich?"

Fay hated the question, but she couldn't very well take out her wounds on the boy. "Yes, Jeff, she was.

Very rich. But money isn't the most important thing in the world. It won't buy good health or happiness."

"Yeah, but it sure would buy a lot of Nintendo games!" he enthused.

She laughed despite herself. But Donavan was silent all through the meal, and afterward.

While Fay was washing dishes, he came into the room. His hands were dangling from the thumbs in his jeans pockets, his silver eyes watchful in a face like a carving in a stone cliff.

"I heard you call Abby Ballenger just before supper. Why? Did you tell her you were resigning?" he asked slowly.

"I'm not resigning. You do realize that paperwork and so forth takes time?" she added, playing for time. "I don't automatically inherit. Neither does Uncle Henry."

"You wouldn't have known that by the way he was talking on the way to his house," he reminded her with a calculating smile. "He's already got his money spent. Or he will have, by the time he actually gets it."

She didn't speak. He made her nervous. It was impossible to be in the same room with him and not remember how it had been between them that one night of their honeymoon. Even without the ultimate intimacy, she'd had a taste of Donavan that still could make her head spin. She loved him with all her heart. It wouldn't have mattered if he'd owned several multinational corporations or only a rope and an old

horse. She loved him so much that his circumstances
would never have made any difference. But he didn't
feel the same about her, and she didn't need him to put
it into words. She had money—or so he thought—and
he didn't, so he didn't want her. Nothing would alter
his opinion one iota, and she knew that, too.

"I should have stayed there with you, shouldn't I?"
he asked unexpectedly. "You look worn to a nub, Fay.
All that grief and your uncle to deal with at once. I
suppose all the details were left up to you."

It was a question, she supposed. "Yes," she replied. "Uncle Henry was able to make the funeral arrangements, though, with the attorney's help. I sorted
out the things in the apartment—" She stopped,
blinking to stay the tears. She washed the same plate
again, slowly. "It was so empty without her."

He hesitated. "So was this house, without you in
it," he said gruffly.

She swallowed. She didn't dare turn around.
"Thanks, but you don't have to pretend. I haven't
lived here long enough to make any real difference in
your life, or Jeff's. You're a better cook than I am,
and you've had people to help you straighten up. I'm
just a temporary convenience. Nothing more."

He was conscious of a terrible wounding in her and
in himself. Had he made her feel so inadequate that
she thought he was better off without her than with
her?

"The boy wants to see that new adventure movie that just came out. It's playing at the Longview. Want to come with us?"

"Oh, no, I don't think so," she forced herself to say. "I'm very tired. You two go ahead, and enjoy yourselves. I just want to go to bed and sleep the clock around."

He hesitated. "Fay, we can wait until you're rested."

"I don't like movies, honestly," she said quickly. "But thanks all the same."

He moved closer, his eyes narrow and concerned. "You've had a rough time lately, and I haven't been much help. Listen, Fay . . ."

"I don't need pity," she said, her voice steady despite the turmoil his nearness aroused. She dried her hands and sidestepped away from him. "I'm learning to stand on my own two feet. I won't pretend it's easy, but I think I'm finally getting the hang of it. After the custody hearing next week, I may see about moving back to my apartment house."

"You're assuming that I'll win it," he said formally. "There's a good chance that I won't. And if you tip out the front door hours later, Jeff's stepfather may appeal the court's decision even if I do win. Proof of an unstable home life would cost dearly."

Incredible that he sounded so determined to keep her with him, when she knew that wasn't what he wanted at all. Of course, it was for Jeff's sake. He loved the boy, if he loved no one else.

"All right," she said, sounding and feeling trapped. She sighed deeply. "I'll stay as long as you need me."

"If you stay that long, you'll never leave," he said curtly.

He turned and left the room, with Fay staring after him in a daze, not quite sure that she'd really heard him right. Probably, she thought later, it was only wishful thinking on her part.

They fell into a routine as the days passed. Fay went back to work, despite Donavan's comment that she was taking a job that someone else might really need, and Jeff went to school each day and began to look the very picture of a happy boy.

Fay worked harder than she ever had before, deliberately putting in late hours and paying more attention to detail than ever. Calhoun and Justin Ballenger were complimentary and appreciative of her efforts. Donavan was not.

"You do nothing but work!" he complained one evening when she wasn't working late—a rarity in recent days. "Don't Jeff and I count with you?"

"Uncle Don, Fay has to do her job right," Jeff pointed out. He grinned. "Besides, Mr. Ballenger says she's saved them plenty with all that hard work."

Donavan finished his dessert and reached for the carafe, to pour himself a second cup of coffee. "So I hear."

"You don't work any less hard yourself," Fay accused him. "And I don't complain."

His silver eyes met hers with cold impact. "Most brand-new wives would."

He was making an insinuation that, fortunately, went right over Jeff's head. But Fay knew what he was really saying, and she flushed.

"Yes, well, ours is hardly a normal situation."

"It could be," he said, startling her into looking up. There was no teasing, no mockery in his expression. He was deadly serious.

Fay flushed. "There's no time."

He lifted an eyebrow. "I beg your pardon?"

The flush grew worse. Jeff finished the last of his dessert and excused himself. "I want to get out of the line of fire," he said dryly, and closed the door into the living room. Seconds later, the TV blared out.

"Turn that damned thing down!" Donavan raged.

"You bet!" Jeff said irrepressibly and barely touched the knob.

Donavan, placated, was still glaring at Fay. "We're husband and wife," he reminded her. "There's no reason on earth that you can't share a bed with me."

"There's a very good one," she differed. She put down her napkin. "When Jeff's situation is resolved,

I don't plan to stay here any longer than I have to. I won't risk getting pregnant.''

His face drained of color. He looked . . . wounded. Cut to the bone. Fay felt sick at the careless comment when she saw its results. She hadn't even meant it. She loved him, but he only wanted her. She was fighting for her emotional survival, with the few weapons she had left.

''I didn't mean that,'' she said stiffly, averting her eyes. ''Not like it sounded. But you must realize I'm right. A baby right now would . . . would complicate things.''

''You don't think children can be prevented?'' he asked with cutting sarcasm.

She lifted her eyes to his. ''I won't be around that much longer,'' she said quietly. ''I realize I must be stifling your sex life, and I'm sorry, but very soon I'll be gone and you can . . . Your life can get back to normal.''

He grew colder in front of her eyes. He threw down his napkin and slowly got to his feet. ''So that's what it's come down to in your mind. I'm hot for a woman and you're someone I can use in the meantime, until I'm free.''

She went scarlet. ''You can't pretend you feel anything other than desire for me,'' she said proudly. ''After all, I'm rich.''

His gaze averted to the table. He stared at it for a long moment. ''Yes.'' He'd almost forgotten. Memories came back, of his father's greed, the censure after Rand Langley's second wife had committed suicide.

He left without another word. After a few minutes, Fay got up and cleared away the dishes. Well, what had she expected him to do, deny it? She laughed at her own folly and then had to bite back tears.

The court hearing was only two days away now, and both Jeff and Donavan were looking as if the pressure of it was giving them some problems.

Fay went by the video rental store and found three movies that would probably appeal to the two men in her life—both of whom were adventure fans—and presented them after supper.

"Wow!" Jeff enthused. "I've wanted to see these for ages! Thanks, Aunt Fay!"

"I didn't think you liked adventure films," Donavan remarked.

She shrugged. "I can take them or leave them. But I thought they might take Jeff's mind off court." She looked up at him curiously. "Have you heard anything from his stepfather, even through the lawyer?"

He shook his head. "It wouldn't surprise me to find that he's having us watched, though."

"Why?"

"Looking for anything to further his case." He laughed coldly. "It would be like him."

"Neither of us has been indiscreet," she reminded him primly, but with a nervous glance.

He glared at her. "I told you, I don't have women on the side. As long as we're married, you're it."

She averted her face. "Thank you."

"I hope that I can expect the same courtesy?"

Her eyes on his face were explosive and expressive. "You don't have to worry about that. I don't attract too many men now that I'm not rich anymore!"

The slip caught Donavan's attention. "You just inherited a fortune," he reminded her.

"Oh. Oh, yes," she faltered. She turned away quickly. "Nevertheless, I'm not going to break my wedding vows."

"I never thought you would, Fay," he said unexpectedly. He moved close behind her and caught her waist gently in his lean hands. "You needn't flinch like that." His voice was quiet, tender. "I may be a 14-karat heel, but I wouldn't hurt you physically."

"I know that," she said breathlessly. "And I don't think you're a heel. You love Jeff very much, don't you?"

He heard the jerky sound of her breathing and moved even closer, his powerful body all but wrapping around hers from behind. His face eased down so that his cheek was against hers, his warm breath sighing out at the corner of her mouth.

Her cold hands rested uneasily atop his, tremulous as the spell of his nearness made her pulse race wildly.

"It's easy to love a child," he said heavily. "Even a neglected, temperamental one. A child accepts love and returns it. Adults know better than to trust it."

"I see."

His hands tightened and his mouth dropped to her soft neck, pressing there hotly. "You see nothing," he said huskily. "Lift your mouth. I want it."

She started to protest, but the stark need of his mouth silenced her. His lips parted hers ruthlessly. He whipped her around against him, his body hardening as he held hers possessively to it. He groaned softly, and the sound made her even weaker.

With a tiny sigh, her mind let go and made her vulnerable in his arms. She reached up, opening her mouth to the rough, insistent probing of his tongue. The sensations he was causing made her knees tremble, and eventually it was only the crush of his arms that kept her on her feet at all.

The sudden silence in the living room was as blatant as a gunshot. Donavan reluctantly lifted his head just as Jeff's footsteps impinged on the silence.

Fay tried to pull back, but Donavan wouldn't let go. "He isn't blind," he said unsteadily. "Stay put."

She didn't quite grasp what he meant until he moved deliberately against her, making her realize at once that his hunger for her was blatant and easily seen.

She subsided and laid her cheek on his broad chest, relaxing against him as Jeff pushed open the kitchen door, and made an embarrassed sound.

"Sorry," he faltered. "I needed a soft drink."

"Help yourself," Donavan said, chuckling. "We are married, you know," he added, lightening the atmosphere.

"It's about time you started acting like you were," Jeff murmured with a grin. He got his soft drink and closed the door behind him with a faint wink at Fay.

"I'll remind you of the same thing," he told her when he stepped back and her face flamed before she was able to avert her eyes. "And you've seen me with a hell of a lot less on, in this condition."

"Will you stop?" she moaned.

"You're very easily embarrassed for an old married woman." His eyes narrowed as he paused long enough to light a cigar. He watched her closely. "I'll keep you from getting pregnant. I want you in my bed tonight. Hear me out," he added when she started to speak. "Sophistication is the one thing you can't fake. If even Jeff realizes we aren't living like married people, his stepfather might realize it as well. We could still lose Jeff."

She hesitated. "I realize that."

"You can pretend all you like," he added, "but you want what I can give you in bed. You're as excited right now as you were in the motel room the night after we married. The difference," he said sensually, "is that now we can experience each other totally, Fay. I can satisfy you totally."

Her lips parted. She could still feel him on them, taste him on them. He looked at her and knew, at once, that she was totally at his mercy.

Slowly he put out the cigar. He opened the door. "Jeff, we're going to have an early night. Bed by eleven, got that?"

"What? Oh, sure, Uncle Don," he said distractedly, his eyes on the TV screen. "Sleep well."

"You, too."

He closed the door and caught Fay's cold hand in his. He tugged her with him to the hall door, opened and closed it behind them, and then led her into the darkness of his own bedroom.

He closed that door, and locked it. Seconds later, in the warm dark, Fay felt him lever down completely against her, pushing her back against the cool wood of the door as the heat of his muscular body overwhelmed her.

While he kissed her, his hands slid under the dress she was wearing and played havoc with her aroused body. Long before he began to take her clothes off, she was barely able to stand alone.

Later, she lay quietly, trembling, in his bed while he removed his own clothes. She could barely see him in the faint light from the window, but what she saw was devastating, and her breath caught.

"You know what to expect already," he whispered as he eased down beside her and began to arouse her all over again. "Except that this time," he whispered into her mouth, "I'm going to fill you..."

She cried out. His mouth hurt, his body was hard and heavy, but she didn't notice, didn't care. She welcomed the warm weight of him, the fierce passion of his mouth and hands. She even welcomed the faint flash of pain when he came into her, her body arching up to receive him, her eyes wide with shock and awe as he slowly completed his possession and then paused, hovering with her on the brink of some sensual precipice.

One lean hand had her hip in its steely grasp. He looked at her, breathing unsteadily, his silver eyes glistening with excitement, beads of sweat on his lean, swarthy face.

His hand contracted and he moved, sensually, just enough to make her feverishly aware of how intimate their embrace was.

She caught her breath and he laughed, deep in his throat.

"Yes," he whispered roughly. "You didn't realize just how intimate it was going to be, did you, little one?"

"N-no," she got out. She looked at him in astonishment, feeling him in every cell of her body. It was embarrassing, shocking, to talk to a man in the throes of such intimacy. And he was laughing. "It isn't funny," she choked.

"I'm not laughing because I'm amused," he whispered, and bent to nibble with barely contained hunger at her softly swollen lips. His hips curled down into hers and lifted, creating a sudden sensual vortex that coaxed a cry of shocked pleasure from her lips. "I'm laughing because you're the most sensual little virgin in the world, and because despite the newness and fear, you're giving yourself to me without a single inhibition. Lift your hips. Let me feel you as close as you can get."

She obeyed him, her body on fire. Her dreams had never been so explicit. Her nails bit into his broad shoulders as he began to move with exquisite delicacy.

"I may be a little rough with you now," he whispered into her mouth. "Don't be afraid of my passion. If you give yourself to it, to me, I'll give you a kind of pleasure you can't even imagine. Match me. Match my rhythm. Don't pull back. That's it." His teeth clenched and he groaned as his body stiffened. "Oh, God, I'm losing it . . . !"

He did. He lost it completely, before he could give her the time she needed to experience fulfillment. He arched above her, his face contorted and terrible in its unearthly pleasure, and he bit off something explicit and harsh as he gave in to the silky convulsions.

"I'm sorry," he whispered, lying drained and heavy over her. "My God, I'm so sorry!"

"Sorry that you made love to me?" she asked in a curious whisper.

"Sorry that I didn't satisfy you!"

"Oh." She stroked his dark hair gently. "You mean, the way you did the night we were married?" She smiled. "Now you can, can't you?"

He stared at her poleaxed. "You think that what just happened was only for my benefit?"

She frowned. "Wasn't it?"

He pulled her close and his arms tightened. "You're one in a million, do you know that? Lift this leg...yes!"

She gasped as his body suddenly became part of hers. She hadn't expected this again so soon. Weren't men supposed to be incapable for several minutes after intimacy?

He moved slowly, exquisitely, and her breath caught. She clung to him, as the most astounding sensations worked through her tightening body.

"Donavan," she began, and suddenly cried out at the unexpected spasm of staggering pleasure.

"Be quiet, sweetheart," he whispered at her mouth, his hips moving with more insistence now, more purpose. "Hold on tight. Yes, Fay, feel it, yes...yes!"

She wept brokenly as the pleasure burst inside her like an overfilled balloon. She had no control whatsoever over her body or the vicious contractions that convulsed her under his openly watchful eyes.

He whispered to her, words of encouragement, praise, flattery, while his mouth touched quickly over her flushed, taut face. It went on and on. She shuddered and clung, convulsed and clung, experiencing sensations beyond her wildest dreams of perfection.

At last, the world stopped rocking and whirling around her. She trembled helplessly in the aftermath, drenched in sweat, weeping softly from the onrush of pleasure and its abrupt loss.

Donavan cradled her in his hard arms, smoothing back her damp hair as he comforted her.

"This," he said after a few minutes, "is what intimacy really is."

"I thought...before, at the motel..." She couldn't quite find the words.

"An alternate way of making love," he said quietly. "But nothing like the real thing. Was it, Fay?"

He wasn't mocking, or teasing. His voice was soft and deep and matter-of-fact.

"We...were like one person," she whispered into his cool, hair-roughened chest.

"Yes." His cheek moved against hers and he kissed her, very gently.

Her body felt pleasantly tired. She went boneless against him and slid even closer, her legs tangling with his. "Can I stay with you?" she asked drowsily.

His arms tightened. "Let me put it this way—just try to get away."

She smiled sleepily. "I don't think I want to."

He bit the lobe of her ear softly. "I want you again, right now," he said huskily, feeling her heart jump under his palm. "But we'll wait until in the morning. It didn't hurt? Even the first time?"

"No," she lied, and snuggled closer. It hadn't hurt very much. And the second time had been heaven.

"Fay," he said hesitantly. His fingers threaded through her soft hair. "Fay, I forgot to use anything."

She didn't stir, or answer. He looked down and realized belatedly that she was asleep.

He bent and kissed her closed eyelids. "Maybe it's just as well that you didn't hear me," he whispered. His lean hand found her soft belly and rested there possessively. "You'd love a baby, Fay. So would I. Maybe it's already happened. If it has, perhaps I can convince you that it would be a bonus, not a complication."

Fay was wavering between consciousness and sleep. She heard Donavan say something about a bonus, but her mind was already headed for oblivion. She clung closer and gave in to it.

Chapter Nine

Fay was humming softly to herself when Donavan came in from the barn. He'd gone out without waking her, and she was disappointed. She'd been hoping that the night before might have coaxed him to want her again, but obviously that hope had been doomed.

She stopped humming when he walked in, her eyes a little shy and nervous. "Good morning," she began, searching for the right words.

He paused in the doorway, and he could have been playing poker for all the expression in his face. Her stiff composure told him things he didn't want to know. He'd pleased her in the night. He'd hoped that things would change between them now that she knew what married life could be. But he wasn't reassured.

She looked uncomfortable and poised to run. If she felt anything for him, it didn't show. And he needed some reassurance before he paraded his own feelings in front of her; his pride would take a mighty blow if she didn't care anymore.

"Good morning," he replied with equal formality. "Breakfast ready?"

"Almost."

He turned. "I'll call Jeff."

And not a word was said, either about the night before, or about what he felt. Fay watched him surreptitiously, hoping to see some flicker of warmth in those silver eyes. But they never met hers. He was polite, nothing more. Fay left the table resolved not to expect anything from that encounter in the darkness the night before. It was just as well, because that night he didn't come near her.

The next morning, they went to church, and then spent a lazy afternoon in front of the television watching old movies. There had hardly been three words spoken in front of Jeff, who looked worried.

"Something bothering you?" Donavan asked curtly after supper.

Jeff looked uncomfortable. "Yes, sir. Sort of."

"What is it?"

"It's you and Aunt Fay," he said miserably, wincing at Fay's shock and Donavan's quick anger. "I'm sorry, but if you two go into court tomorrow looking like you do right now, I guess I'll be back in military school by the next morning. Could you pretend to like each other, just while we're in court?''

"No problem there," Donavan assured him. "Now you'd better get your bath and go to sleep. We've got a big day ahead tomorrow.''

When he left the room, Donavan got up and turned off the television. His eyes lingered on Fay's flushed cheeks for a few seconds before he spoke.

"He's dead right," he told her. "If we don't present a united front, he won't be able to stay here.''

"I know." She folded her hands in her lap and clenched them, staring at her nails. "I don't want him to have to leave, Donavan, whatever you think.''

His broad shoulders lifted and fell in an offhand gesture. He lit a cigar and stared at its tip. "I shouldn't have lost my head night before last," he said tersely. "It made things worse between us.''

She didn't know how to answer that. She picked at one of her fingernails and didn't look up. "It was my fault, too.''

"Was it? You didn't seduce me, honey," he drawled.

She sighed heavily. "I'm not on the pill," she said.

He hesitated. "Yes, I know.''

"And you . . . well, you didn't do anything . . .''

"That's right," he replied. "Keep going.''

She cleared her throat, glancing up at him. "You might have made me pregnant.''

One corner of his mouth curved gently. "There's an old family christening gown around here somewhere. My great-grandmother made the lace it's edged in. There's a high chair and even a cradle that date back to the first settlers in Jacobsville."

Fay's green eyes softened as they met his. Her cheeks warmed as she looked at him. "I...I have a baptismal set, too. The furniture's all gone. But there's one antique that Great-Aunt Tessie kept—a silver baptismal bowl. I saved it from the auction."

The mention of her deceased relative made his expression become grim. He averted his face and smoked his cigar, still pacing slowly. "You inherited a lot of money," he said. "Can't you keep the furniture, or don't you want it?"

"I have no place for it in my apartment," she said simply.

He spun on his heel, glaring at her. "This is your home. There's no way on earth you're leaving here until I know if you're pregnant."

She started. "It's unlikely..."

"Why? Because it was the first time?" he asked with mocking amusement.

His sophisticated attitude angered her. "Can't we talk about something else?" she asked stiffly.

"Sure." He raised the cigar to his firm lips. He felt optimistic for the first time. She still reacted to him. She couldn't hide the way he affected her. It made him feel proud to realize that she was as helplessly attracted to him as he was to her.

Now, if only her heart was involved . . .

"Why don't you sleep with me tonight?" he asked sensuously. "After all, one more time isn't going to make much difference now."

"You don't want me to stay here," she said. "I don't want a child who has to grow up without his father."

"I didn't say I didn't want you to stay here," he returned.

"You did so!" she raged, standing. "You said that you didn't want me anymore because my great-aunt died and left me rich again! You let me go to Florida all by myself—"

"Not quite. Henry went with you," he pointed out.

She continued as if he hadn't interrupted "—and then you said I could find somewhere else to live!"

"I didn't say that," he murmured dryly. "Surely not?"

"Yes, you did!"

"That was before I slept with you, of course," he pointed out, letting his eyes punctuate the flat statement. "Now I'm hopelessly addicted."

"Any woman would do," she muttered.

"Not really, or I'd have had a few in the past year or so. I'd all but lost interest in sex until you came along and knocked my legs out from under me."

"A likely story, after the things you did to me night before last...!"

She stopped very suddenly, her hand going to her mouth as she realized what she'd said. She sat down again, hard.

"I had experience, Fay," he said softly.

She flushed. "I noticed!"

"You might consider that those early encounters made your life a little easier."

She stared at her feet, still smoldering. "You did things to me that I never even read in books."

"I'll tell you a secret, honey," he mused, putting out his cigar before he came to kneel between her legs where she sat rigidly on the sofa. He was almost on a level with her shocked eyes as he looked into them. "I've never done with anyone some of those things I did to you. And never could."

"C-couldn't you?" she whispered.

"No." His hands caught her waist and pulled gently, suddenly overbalancing so that she landed breathlessly on his chest. He rolled, pinning her under him on the big throw rug. As he held her eyes, one long leg inserted itself between both of hers and he moved slowly.

"I want you again. Now," he told her, his body screaming it in the intimate embrace. His lean hand smoothed blatantly over her soft breast and then began to slip buttons out of buttonholes.

"But the door..." she began.

"Isn't closed. I know." He slid his hand inside her bodice and under her soft bra, to find even softer flesh. His fingers gently caressed it, and she arched, gasping. "I'm going to carry you to bed now," he breathed. "And I'm going to do all those things I did two nights ago. Right now."

He got to his feet and picked her up, shifting her gently as he carried her down the long hall and into his bedroom. He placed her on the bedspread and went to close and lock the door. Then he stood at the foot of the bed, his black hair half in his eyes, his face devoid of expression, his body blatantly aroused.

She eased up onto her elbows, feeling feminine and hotly desired, her green eyes lost in the glitter of his gray ones. He nodded slowly. And then he moved toward her.

But just as he reached her, bent over her, warmed her mouth with his breath in a deliciously tense bit of provocation—the telephone rang noisily on the bedside table.

Donavan stared at it blankly, as if for a moment he didn't even realize what was making the noise.

Impatiently he jerked up the receiver and spoke into it.

A familiar, sarcastic voice came over the line—Brad Danner, Jeff's stepfather.

"I'm looking forward to tomorrow, Donavan," he told the angry man on the other end of the line. "If you think that sham marriage is going to make any difference in a custody suit, you're very wrong."

"It isn't a sham marriage," Donavan said tersely, without looking at Fay, who was sitting shocked and disoriented beside him now, on the bed.

"I'll let you prove that tomorrow. Take good care of my stepson, won't you? I'm looking forward to having him home again."

"Yes, it would be something of a luxury, wouldn't it?" Donavan asked icily. "When you stuck him in military school at his first show of spirit."

"One of you in a family is enough," the other man replied, obviously straining to keep his temper. "All my married life, Debbie threw you up to me. Nothing I did was ever right, ever the same thing *you* would have done in my place. My God, you don't now how I hated you!"

"Debbie always had a tendency to romanticize everything," Donavan said curtly. "After Dad died, I was all she had. As for her opinion of you," he added with mocking amusement, "I had nothing to do with it. You were a spineless complainer from day one. And don't tell me the dowry I gave her wasn't the real inducement to get you to the altar. You spent half of it the first week you were married to Debbie—on your mistress!"

The other receiver slammed down. Donavan slowly replaced his, chuckling with bitter amusement.

"Jeff's would-be guardian," he said, nodding toward the telephone. "He fancies himself a man. Imagine that?"

"He might have loved your sister," she began.

"Really? If he did, why was he involved with another woman before, during and after the marriage? The woman he's married to now, by the way. Debbie's insurance money set them up real well. He made sure that Jeff wasn't mentioned as a beneficiary."

"He sounds very mercenary," she said quietly.

"He thinks he can prove that our marriage is a fraud," he said. His eyes narrowed on her face. "It's imperative that we act like lovers. You understand that?"

She nodded. Her eyes fell to his broad chest, where his shirt was unbuttoned over a thick mat of curling black hair.

"I understand." Her lips parted with helpless hunger, but she lowered her eyes so that he wouldn't see how she felt. "That's why you brought me in here, isn't it, Donavan? So that it would show, in court tomorrow, that we'd been intimate."

He hesitated, but only for an instant. "Yes," he said curtly. "That's right. I wanted to make you look loved, so that I wouldn't risk losing Jeff."

"I see."

Her defeated expression made him wild. "He might run away if he gets sent back, don't you see? He's high-strung. I can't let that happen. He's all the family I have left in the world, Fay!''

She stood up with a long, gentle sigh. ''Funny,'' she said as she turned. ''Once upon a time, I thought I was part of your family. It just goes to show how money can warp you. Being rich must have made me stupid.''

He rammed his hands into his pockets. He felt guilty, and he didn't like it. She was rich. She had the world. She didn't need a poor husband and a ready-made family, anyway. Even *if* he wanted her for keeps, which he didn't. He had one scandal to live down. He couldn't take another.

He only hoped he hadn't made her pregnant in that feverish coupling. It would make her life impossible, because he knew he'd never be able to turn his back on his own child. She'd be trapped then, and so would he.

''It's just as well that Brad interrupted us,'' he said tersely, thinking aloud. ''I've been unforgivably careless about taking precautions. It's just as well if we don't take any more risks. I'll see you in the morning, Fay.''

It was a dismissal. He looked as unapproachable as a porcupine. Fay couldn't understand why he'd bothered trying to seduce her in the first place. Now he seemed concerned about not making her pregnant. She left him there and went to bed, hurt and bitter and totally confused.

She dressed very carefully for court the next morning, in her off-white suit and leather high heels. She carried the one designer purse she had left, and wore a very becoming and very expensive spring hat. She looked what she was—a young woman with breeding who'd been raised to be a lady.

Donavan, in his pale gray suit, was openly appreciative of the way she looked. In fact, he could hardly keep his eyes off her.

"You look . . . lovely," he said.

She managed a cool smile. "Why thank you, darling," she said, playing her part to the hilt. Only her eyes gave the show away, because they were like two green pieces of ice. His hot-cold attitude had worn her out. She was giving up all hope of a happy marriage, but first she was going to help Jeff out of his predicament. It was a matter of honor. She'd given her word.

"Very nice," he replied curtly. "You'll convince anyone who doesn't look at your face too closely."

"I can handle that." She pulled the hat's matching veil down over her nose. "Now. One wife, properly accounted for, ready to go on stage."

He stiffened and turned away, his anger evident and blatant.

Jeff came out of his bedroom in a suit. He looked from Fay to Donavan and grimaced. "Well, I guess I'm as ready as I'll ever be, but I'm sure not looking forward to it."

"Neither are we," Donavan said. "All the more reason to get it over with as soon as possible. Try not to worry," he added gently, placing an affectionate hand on the boy's stooped shoulder. "And stand up straight. Don't let him think he's got you buffaloed."

"Yes, Uncle Don."

He herded Fay and Jeff out to the car and drove them to the county courthouse in a silence filled with worried looks and cigar smoke.

Brad Danner wasn't at all what Fay had expected. He was short and redheaded and looked as if he had a massive ego.

"So you're the brand-new Mrs. J. D. Langley," Brad said mockingly, shaking off the firm hand of a suited man who was probably his attorney. "Well, it won't work. You might as well go back to whichever bar he found you at and throw in your chips. You'll never pull this off. I've got too much on you!"

"Have you indeed?" Fay asked, enjoying herself now. "Actually, Donavan did find me in a bar." She leaned closer. "But I didn't work there."

"Oh, of course not," he agreed amiably, and laughed as he turned back to the bleached blonde with the overlipsticked mouth who was obviously pregnant and almost certainly his wife.

Donavan motioned for Fay to sit down at the table with him. Jeff had already been taken away by a juvenile officer for the course of the hearing.

Formalities had to be observed. Once those were out of the way, Donavan's attorney—an elderly man with keen eyes and alarming dignity—offered Brad's attorney the opportunity to present his case first.

Donavan looked nervous, but Mr. Flores only smiled and winked.

Brad's attorney got up and made a long speech about the things Brad had done for his stepson, most recently having enrolled him in a top-flight educational facility, which would lead him to an admirable career.

"We do concede that Mr. Danner has no blood relationship with the boy, as does Mr. Langley. However, despite his hasty marriage in an attempt to present a stable home environment, Mr. Langley overlooked one small detail. He neglected to keep his new wife close to home."

Fay and Donavan exchanged puzzled glances. The opposing attorney opened his briefcase and dragged out several photographs of Fay with her uncle on the way to Florida, and at Tessie's apartment, where they'd stayed until the funeral was over.

"This is the kind of monkey business the new Mrs. Langley gets up to when her husband's back is turned," the attorney said haughtily, glaring at Fay as if she were a fallen woman. "Hardly a moral example for a young boy!"

Donavan chuckled.

"You find these photographs amusing, Mr. Langley? You had been married for only a matter of days, I believe, when Mrs. Langley and her gentleman friend flew to Florida alone?"

"You aren't from here, are you?" Donavan asked the attorney. "And apparently neither is your private detective."

"He isn't a private detective, he's a friend of mine who used to be in intelligence work during the Korean War," Brad said stiffly. "But you won't lie your way out of this. That man in the photographs is . . . !"

". . . my uncle," Fay said. She glanced at Judge Ridley, who was an old friend of her family—and who was also trying not to break up.

"I'm afraid so," Judge Ridley agreed, wiping the unjudicial smile off his face. "I've known Henry for years."

"If he's her uncle, why doesn't he have the same surname she does?" the other attorney argued.

"Henry is Fay's mother's brother," Judge Ridley explained. "Surely your detective checked?"

"He said Donavan had probably found her at a bar," Brad began.

"Mrs. Langley and her uncle went to Florida to make the final arrangements for Mrs. Langley's great-aunt," Donavan's attorney clarified. "As for your friend's assertion that Mrs. Langley worked in a bar, let me assure you that nothing could be farther from the truth. In point of fact, she was a debutante. And now, with the death of her great-aunt, she stands to inherit a large share of the estate.''

Brad looked sick.

"I am also reliably told," Judge Ridley interrupted, "by the young boy whose custody is in question, that his uncle and Mrs. Langley have a warm, loving relationship, which gives him a much-needed feeling of security. Your accusation that the marriage is fraudulent hardly concurs with the home life the young man describes.''

"He'd do anything to get Jeff, even pretending to be happily married. Ask him if he loves her," he challenged the judge. "Go ahead! He never lies. Make him tell her how he really feels about her!''

Fay stood up. "I know how my husband feels about me, Mr. Danner," she said stiffly. "I also know how you feel about him. Jeff is only a pawn to you. But he's a flesh-and-blood boy to Donavan. They're very happy together. Jeff will get a good education and caring company, and it won't be in a military school where he isn't even allowed weekend visits home more than twice a year! If you wanted him so badly, why send him away in the first place?''

"A good question," the judge agreed. He stared at Brad, who was slowly turning red. "Answer it, please.''

"My wife is pregnant," Brad said shortly. "Jeff makes her nervous. Isn't that right, honey?''

"I fail to see why you sought custody, Mr. Danner," the judge persisted.

"Oh, tell him, Bradley," the blonde muttered. She sanded a nail to perfection. "He only wants the insurance money. He's afraid if he loses custody, he'll have to give Jeff his share of it, and he's already spent it."

"You idiot!" Brad raged at his wife.

"What's so terrible about the truth?" she asked with careless unconcern. "You were so scared of your brother-in-law finding out. Well, now he knows. Big deal. It's only a thousand dollars, anyway. If you hadn't bought that stupid boat, you could have afforded to pay it back."

The courtroom erupted. Before the fur stopped flying, Fay got a glimpse of the real Brad Danner, and she was very sorry for his second wife. By the time Fay and Donavan left the courtroom, with custody of Jeff and the promise of repayment of the insurance money Jeff should have had, Fay's head was whirling.

"Aunt Fay, I'm so relieved!" Jeff laughed, and hugged her impulsively. "I can stay, isn't it radical?"

"Just radical," she agreed happily.

"And you and Uncle Don fooled them all," he added. "Everybody thought you were the most devoted couple anywhere!"

"That was the joke of the century, all right," Fay said quietly, and met Donavan's angry eyes over Jeff's head. "Congratulations. You've got what you wanted."

"Yes," he said. "I've got everything I wanted."

She smiled coolly, grateful for the veil that hid her sadness, and put an affectionate arm around Jeff as they walked toward the car.

Donavan walked a little behind them. He didn't know how he felt exactly, but elated wouldn't have covered it. He was glad to have Jeff with him, of course, but in the process he was certain to lose Fay.

That shouldn't bother him. Fay was rich; he wasn't. Their life-styles would never mix, and everyone would think that he'd married her for her money. Hell, they probably thought it already. He laughed at his own folly. Even if he divorced her, they'd say he was after a big cash settlement in return for her freedom. They'd say like father, like son.

Suddenly the public censure that had worried him so much before fell into place. If he knew what his motives were, did it really matter what a few small-minded people thought? It was usually the hypocrites who gossiped, anyway—the people who lived public lives of high morality and private lives of glaring impurity. The few friends he had wouldn't sit in judgment on him. So why was he agonizing over his plight?

He glanced at Fay hungrily. Hell, he wanted her. He'd grown used to having her around the house. He enjoyed watching her stumbling attempts to cook edible meals. He liked the smell of her perfume when he stood close to her, and the way she fussed over him and Jeff, as if it really mattered to her that something might happen to one of them. He liked her, most especially, sliding under his body in bed, giving him her warmth and exquisite sensuality, giving him ecstasy that even in memory could make him weak in the knees. He wanted to stay with her. He wanted a child with her. Was it too late? Had he done too much damage?

"Suppose we stop off at the pizza place and get a supreme to go?" Jeff suggested. "After all, we are celebrating."

"Good idea. We'll give Aunt Fay the night off," Donavan agreed.

"He's just tired of bouncing biscuits and black steak," she told Jeff with a sigh. "I guess one well-cooked meal won't kill us all."

Jeff laughed, but Fay didn't. Now that Donavan had Jeff, she wondered how much time she had left until Donavan wanted her out of his life for good.

Chapter Ten

The pizza was delicious. Fay enjoyed it as much as the rest of the family seemed to, but her heart wasn't in the celebration. She wanted to stand up and scream that life was unfair, that she'd been shortchanged all the way around. She'd always had money. But she'd never had love. Now it seemed that she didn't have either. Great-Aunt Tessie's legacy would be nice, but it would hardly allow her to give up her job. With some careful investing, it would grow, as long as she could live on what she made.

She worried about that for the rest of the day, trying to put on a happy face for Jeff. But Donavan saw through it. He joined her in the porch swing while Jeff played with one of three new snow-white puppies in the barn.

"We won," he reminded her as he smoked his cigar. Like her, he'd changed into casual clothes—jeans and a cotton shirt. He propped one booted foot on the swing and glanced down at her. "Aren't you glad?"

"Of course," she said absently. "I know how worried Jeff was."

He stared out over the horizon. "There really wasn't too much to worry about," he mused. "I had a contact of mine feed his Korean War veteran buddy a few scandalous facts about you and Uncle Henry. It's not my fault the man took it for gospel and didn't double check. His loss, my gain."

"Donavan!" she burst out. "That's devious!"

"That's how I am when people I love get threatened." He looked down at her. "I'll fight under the table, any way at all, to win when someone else's life depends on it. I couldn't let that strutting rooster get Jeff. It wasn't a tug of war with me—it was Jeff's whole life."

"I know he appreciates what you've done for him."

"I don't imagine you do. I'm sorry to have made you look, even temporarily, like a fallen angel. But I had no choice."

"I understood. Even the judge was having a hard time keeping a straight face."

"Where do we go from here, Fay?" he asked solemnly.

She listened to the creak as the wooden swing pulled against the chains rhythmically.

"I'll stay until your brother-in-law is safely back home and over his defeat," she said. "We've already discussed where I'll go."

"No we haven't," he disagreed. "You said you were going to move back to the apartment house and I said you weren't. My God, buy yourself a place, why don't you?"

Her hands clasped together painfully. Didn't he know he was tearing the heart out of her?

"I might, later on."

She wasn't giving an inch. He couldn't tell anything by her voice or her expression.

"You could stay on here," he remarked casually. "There's plenty of room. Jeff likes you. So does Bee."

"I've burned up enough good food already."

"We haven't complained."

She smiled to herself. Amazingly they hadn't. Only three days ago, Jeff had complimented her on one small side dish that was actually fit to eat.

"I might get the hang of it one day."

He studied his boot. "How about getting the hang of making formula and changing dirty diapers?" he asked, his eyes on the horizon.

She hesitated. He sounded...serious. "What do you mean?"

He shrugged. He lifted the cigar to his mouth and took a draw from it, blowing out a large cloud of pungent smoke. "I mean, suppose we stayed married. If you'd let me, I think I could make you pregnant eventually. We could raise a family, give Jeff a stable environment to finish growing up in."

She studied his profile. Nothing there. He looked as formidable as he had the first time she'd ever seen him. Just as handsome, too, she thought wistfully.

He glanced down and saw that wistfulness and one eyebrow went up. He looked at her openly now, from her forehead down to her mouth and back up to her eyes. "You're thinner. I've been cruel to you, Fay. Give me a chance to put things right."

"By making me pregnant?" she asked with pretended lightness.

"If it's what you want, yes. If not, we can put if off for a few years. You're still very young, little one. You might like to go to college or do some traveling before you get tied down with children."

"I've already done my traveling, and I don't want to go to college. I have a nice job already."

"You can resign from that," he said. "You don't need it."

She stared at him for a long moment, until he scowled. "Actually," she confessed, "I'm afraid I do."

"If you just want a way to get out of the house..."

She rested her cool fingers atop the lean hand that was propped on his jean-clad knee. "Donavan, I'm not exactly going to inherit a fortune."

"Yes, I know. Henry said you'll only get about a third, when it's all wrapped up. It doesn't matter," he said doggedly, averting his face. "I don't give a damn what people think anymore. I don't know now why I ever did. I'm not like my father. I married you for Jeff's sake, not because I stood to gain a fortune."

She felt the impact of that statement down to her toes. If only he'd married her for love of her. She sighed, audibly.

He tilted her face up to his. "What a wistful little sound," he said quietly. "You don't like thinking that I only married you for Jeff. You liked it even less when you thought it was for money."

"It doesn't bother me," she lied.

"Sure it does," he countered quietly. "I wanted you," he said softly. "You knew that already, I imagine."

"Yes."

"You wanted me back. I didn't have to coerce you into my bed. You came willingly."

She flushed and looked down at the lean fingers that slowly wrapped around hers in a close embrace. "It was new and...exciting."

"More than just exciting, I think, little one." His voice was soft, deep, sensual. "I lost you for a few seconds just as I fulfilled you. It made me feel pretty good to know I could give you that much pleasure."

"As you said," she swallowed, "you've had a lot of experience."

"I've had a lot of *bodies*," he said with faint cynicism. "Just that, Fay, a lot of bodies in the dark. I went through the motions and learned the right moves. But it was nothing like what I had with you, even on our wedding night, when my hands were all but tied. I knew then that it was more than physical attraction. But I knew it for certain when I put you on that plane to Florida and let you walk away from me. I didn't sleep all night, for thinking how cruel I'd been. You loved Tessie, and I'd given you no comfort, no support at all. I'm sorry for that. I owed you more than that."

"You owed me nothing," she told him dully. "We got married for Jeff, that's all."

His free hand spread against her soft cheek and lifted her face. "Haven't you been listening to me at all?" he asked softly.

"Yes," she said nervously. "You've got me on your conscience."

"Fay, listen with your heart, not your ears," he replied. He searched her face with eyes that adored it. "Can't you see it? Can't you feel it? Fay, can't you put your mouth on mine and taste it...?"

He pulled her lips under his and kissed her with such tenderness that she felt her body ripple with sheer pleasure.

His tongue probed inside her mouth, increasing the heat, making her moan. While he built the kiss, he lifted and turned her, so that she was lying completely in his arms, pressed close against the heat of his muscular chest.

Unseen, his lean hand eased inside her shirt and began to trace the warm, taut contours of her breast until he made the nipple go hard against his fingers.

He lifted his head minutes later, and looked down at her swollen mouth and dazed eyes before his gaze dropped to the taut nipple so evident under the thin fabric.

"You look as out of control as I feel," he said huskily, his gray eyes pure silver in the daylight. "If we were alone, I wouldn't even bother to strip you. I'd just get the necessary things out of the way and I'd take you like a tornado."

She shivered, pressing her hot face into his throat.

"Want it like that?" he whispered at her ear. "Rough and quick and blazing hot?" He glanced over her head at Jeff, who was sprawled in the aisle of the barn playing with the dogs while one of Donavan's older hands watched him.

Donavan stood up abruptly and put Fay on her feet. Catching the older hand's attention, he indicated that he wanted him to keep an eye on Jeff. The cowhand nodded, grinned and waved. Then Donavan turned back to Fay, his eyes glittery with intent.

"Oh...we can't," she faltered as he came toward her and she began backing toward the screen door. "Surely, you were kidding, with Jeff right outside...!"

"Like hell I was kidding," he whispered against her mouth.

He picked her up and carried her straight into his bedroom, pausing just long enough to lock the door before he backed her up against the waist-high vanity and opened the fastening of her jeans.

She gasped and started to protest, but he had her mouth under his, and she couldn't manage speech. She heard the rasp of another zipper, felt him move, and then her jeans slid off her legs. His tongue went roughly into her mouth, in quick, sharp thrusts that were unbelievably arousing.

He lifted her sharply and she felt him suddenly in an intimacy that took her breath. He half lifted her from the vanity, his body levering between her legs while he invaded her with urgent, exquisite mastery. She clung to his neck, feeling the force of his desire with faint awe as she experienced for the first time the unbridled violence of passion.

He wasn't tender, or particularly gentle, but the pleasure that convulsed her was beyond anything he'd given her before. She heard him cry out and felt him tense, then he was heavy in her arms, damp with sweat, trembling faintly from the strength he'd had to exert in the uncomfortable position.

"I like the noises that boil out of you when we make love," he said roughly. "You excite me."

"I can't stop shaking." She laughed shyly.

"Neither can I. We went high this time."

"Yes. Oh, yes!"

He drew back, finally, and looked at her. His face was solemn, his eyes quiet and gentle. He brushed back her damp hair and smiled. "That will have to last us until tonight," he whispered. "Think you can manage?"

"If you can," she teased. His eyes were telling her impossible things, too wonderful for reality. "Am I dreaming?" she asked.

"No, sweetheart. Not at all."

He lifted her, separating his body from hers, and grinned wickedly when she flushed.

"You needn't look so shocked," he chided as he rearranged his own clothing. "Five minutes ago you wouldn't have noticed if we were lying under a table in a restaurant."

"Neither would you!" she accused.

He drew her close and kissed her gently. "That's a fact," he whispered. "God, I love you, Fay."

She stiffened. She couldn't have heard that. She opened her eyes, very wide, and stared at him.

"I haven't given you much reason to believe it, but it's true just the same," he told her quietly. "You're all I want, you and Jeff and however many kids we can have together. If we can't have any, then you and Jeff will more than suffice."

"How long?" she asked gently, desperate now to believe him.

"Since the very first night we met," he replied. "I fought it. God, I did! But in the end, I couldn't do without you. After I made love to you, even light love, I was lost. I knew I'd never be able to let you go."

"Then I inherited Tessie's money," she began.

"I told you. It doesn't matter. I love you. Do whatever you like with your inheritance."

"In that case," she murmured, "I'll put it in the bank for Jeff's education. It should just about cover college."

"Where are we sending him to college—the Waldorf Astoria?"

She smiled warmly, convinced at last that she was awake and aware. "I only inherit part of the proceeds from the sale of her furniture," she told him, and proceeded to explain where the rest of the money was going.

He was surprised, and frankly pleased, that Fay's inheritance wouldn't amount to very much. "She must have been some kind of lady," he remarked.

"She was. A very special one. My share will just about pay for Jeff's college. Now you know why I wouldn't give up my job. I couldn't afford to."

"Just as well the Ballengers made one for you," he murmured. He sighed heavily. "I guess this means that I'll have to start being, ugh, nice to Calhoun."

"That wouldn't hurt," she agreed.

"And your uncle," he added irritably.

"Also a nice touch."

He searched her eyes. "I won't reform completely. You know that. I'm exactly what you see. I won't change."

"Neither will I," she replied. "I might get a little rounder eventually, and have a few gray hairs."

"That's okay," he said pleasantly. "I might do that myself." He pulled her closer. "Fay, I'll never be a rich man. But I'll love you, and take care of you when you need it. If we have nothing else, we'll have each other."

She had to fight tears at the tenderness in his deep voice. She kissed him and then reached up and locked her arms gently around his neck. "I haven't said it," she whispered.

"You said it the night you gave yourself to me completely," he replied, surprised. "Don't you remember? You said it over and over again while you were trembling in my arms at the last."

"I must have been half out of my mind. Loving you does that to me," she whispered with her heart in her eyes.

"And to me," he replied. He bent, fusing her mouth with his in a slow, sweet expression of love.

"Uncle Don!" came a loud voice from below the window.

Donavan groaned. "What now?"

He opened the window and looked down. Jeff was waiting with two of Donavan's foreman's sons, both of whom were carrying fishing poles and tackle boxes.

"Please?" he pleaded with his uncle. "I haven't gotten to go fishing since the last time you took me. I'll bring home supper, honest, can I?"

"Go ahead," Donavan chuckled. "But you'd better bring home supper."

"We'll make sure he does, sir!" one of the older boys called. "Even if we have to swim under his line and hook the fish on it ourselves."

"Thanks!" Jeff laughed.

The boys were out of sight in no time. Donavan closed the window and took the phone off the hook. He moved toward her with a wicked smile.

"Sometimes," he told a breathlessly excited Fay as he began to caress her out of her clothing, "fate can be kind."

A sentiment that Fay would gladly have echoed, except that Donavan's mouth was hard over her own, and seconds later, she was in no condition to think at all....

The next morning, Fay was hard at work when Donavan showed up unexpectedly at the feedlot.

Calhoun, just coming out of his office, grimaced.

"No need to rush, finding excuses to get out of the office right away," Donavan drawled. "I'm reformed. I didn't come to complain. I actually dropped by to see about moving in some more cattle."

Calhoun's eyebrows went up. "You don't say!"

"I just did. While I'm about it, I might add a word of thanks about keeping my wife on," he added ruefully. "We figure her inheritance from her great-aunt will just about put one kid through college. Since we plan on more than our nephew taking up residence, every penny is going to count."

"We like the job Fay does. But it's tough luck," Calhoun ventured, "about the inheritance."

Donavan smiled lazily. "Not in my book. I like the idea of working toward something." He glanced at Fay with his heart in his eyes. "Struggling together brings two people close."

"Indeed it does," Fay agreed with a sigh.

"If you'd like to take your wife to lunch, we might be able to let her off a little early," Calhoun said.

"I was hoping you'd say that," Donavan said and grinned.

He took Fay to the local hamburger joint and they ate cheeseburgers and drank milkshakes until they were pretty well stuffed.

"You won't have an easy life with me," he said when they were outside again. He paused, catching her hand in his to stop and look down at her. "You'll probably always have to work. I can take some of the burden off you at home, because I can cook and do dishes and sweep. But when the kids come along, things could get pretty hectic."

"Am I worried?" she asked, smiling. "Am I complaining? I've got you. I don't need promises, assurances, or anything else. I'm happier than I ever dreamed of being."

"Are you sure?" he asked, and looked worried. "You've always had everything you wanted."

"I still do."

"You know what I mean," he said irritably.

"Yes. Money was nice, but it wasn't particularly easy to cuddle up to. I don't mind living like ordinary working people. In fact," she said honestly, "I really like the challenge. It's nice to feel independent, and to know that you're earning what you have. I never had to earn anything before."

"You're giving me a lot to live up to, honey," he said quietly. "I hope I won't let you down. I'm not the easiest man to live with."

"Yes, you are," she replied. She put her arms around him and pressed close. "As long as I'm holding you, you're the easiest man in the world to get along with. So suppose I just never let go?"

He laughed and let out his breath in a long, contented sigh as he pulled her close and returned the gentle embrace. "I'll tell you something, sweetheart," he murmured contentedly. "That suits me just fine!"

And she never did.

*   *   *   *   *

NORA ROBERTS

Love has a language all its own, and for centuries, flowers have symbolized love's finest expression. Discover the language of flowers—and love—in this romantic collection of 48 favorite books by bestselling author Nora Roberts.

Starting in February 1992, two titles will be available each month at your favorite retail outlet.

In February, look for:

Irish Thoroughbred, Volume #1
The Law Is A Lady, Volume #2

Collect all 48 titles and become fluent in the Language of Love.

LOL192

THE LANGUAGE of LOVE

Silhouette Special Edition

salutes

MOMENTS OF GLORY

from Lindsay McKenna

In a country torn with conflict, in a time of bitter passions,
these brave men and women wage a war against all
odds... and a timeless battle for honor, for fleeting moments
of glory, for the promise of enduring love.

February: RIDE THE TIGER (#721) Survivor Dany Villard is
wise to the love-'em-and-leave-'em ways of war, but
wounded hero Gib Ramsey swears she's captured his
heart... forever.

March: ONE MAN'S WAR (#727) The war raging inside brash
and bold Captain Pete Mallory threatens to destroy him, until
Tess Ramsey's tender love guides him toward peace.

April: OFF LIMITS (#733) Soft-spoken Marine Jim McKenzie
saved Alexandra Vance's life in Vietnam; now he needs her
love to save his honor....

SEMG-1

Silhouette Special Edition

is pleased to present

A GOOD MAN WALKS IN
by Ginna Gray

The story of one strong woman's comeback
and the man who was there for her, Travis McCall,
the renegade cousin to those Blaine siblings,
from Ginna Gray's bestselling trio

FOOLS RUSH IN (#416)
WHERE ANGELS FEAR (#468)
ONCE IN A LIFETIME (#661)

Rebecca Quinn sought shelter at the hideaway on Rincon
Island. Finding Travis McCall—the object of all her childhood
crushes—holed up in the same house threatened to ruin the
respite she so desperately needed. Until their first kiss...
Then Travis set out to prove to his lovely Rebecca that man
can be good and love, sublime.

You'll want to be there when Rebecca's disillusionment turns
to joy.

A GOOD MAN WALKS IN #722

Available at your favorite retail outlet this February.

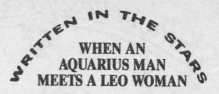